THE HAUNTING OF ORCHARD HILL

A HOPEFUL HORROR NOVEL

SARA CROCOLL SMITH

FUN, FICTION, FANDOM

The Haunting of Orchard Hill
A Hopeful Horror Novel

Copyright © 2022 by Sara Crocoll Smith

Cover design by Janet Linton

Editing by EbookLaunch.com

ISBN 978-1-956546-04-0 (ebook)

ISBN 978-1-956546-05-7 (paperback)

ISBN 978-1-956546-06-4 (hardcover)

ISBN 978-1-956546-07-1 (large print)

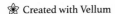 Created with Vellum

To my son

Concerned about her mother's unsettling phone calls, Samantha returns home from abroad to find the curtains drawn and the windows nailed shut.

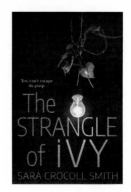

Is dementia causing her mother's strange behavior or something much more sinister?

Claustrophobic humidity... creeping ivy... dark secrets...

Samantha's been the perfect daughter her entire life. As she uncovers what lies at the heart of her childhood home, she'll never be the same again.

Visit SaraCrocollSmith.com/Ivy to get the free short story "The Strangle of Ivy."

1

Nina wasn't sure how long her eyes had been open. She felt like she'd been staring at his face forever. John exhaled, breath stale with last night's beers. His stern mouth seemed softer when illuminated by the sliver of moonlight cast through their crooked bedroom blinds.

Her jaw ached, and the swelling around her eye had dimmed her vision. By inches, she eased her feet out from beneath the covers. The air conditioning turned on with a loud whir, and her nerves rang. She froze as John's eyes fluttered.

With a hitching breath, he inhaled and paused —they both stopped breathing. In the space between breaths, Nina considered tucking her lower half back into bed, pretending as if nothing ever happened, that she'd never intended—

Then she saw the dark spot on her pillow— crimson, she could tell, and sure to leave a stain. Nina pushed up, careful not to let the bed springs move or bounce as the rest of her rose from bed.

On soft feet across their thick, matted rug, Nina stole out of the room and down the hall, careful to pick her way over John's haphazardly strewn uniform, badge, and holster. Above, the rain ceased its soft patter across their sagging roof. These waning days of spring blurred together, with not much to mark this night as different than any other.

Nina had already tallied in her head a million times the things that needed to be packed. Only the essentials—the lightest things that would get her through until she and Holden were safely away. Two suitcases she could carry, one in each hand, while still managing to hold her baby boy. It took her longer than she thought it would to prepare, but within a half-hour's time, she was done. Only one vital task remained before she could leave.

She stood in front of Holden's door, holding her breath. The house was silent. She wished it were louder. Where was the soft murmur of the air conditioner now? Where was the loud creak of the pipes? Where was the hiss and chirping of nightlife to cover her sounds and tracks? She needed to slip inside this room and gather her precious cargo, but it was only one door down from *him*.

Nina gulped.

Sweat gathered at the small of her back, and her hands were more than clammy. She wiped them on her faded jeans. Her nerves gathered steel at the sound of a soft whimper, verging on a cry, on the other side of the door. Nina grasped the doorknob and twisted as even and as steady as she could.

She hadn't turned on any lights since her eyes were still adjusted to the dark. She walked into the room, to the edge of his crib. He stood on unsteady feet, looking up at her with doleful eyes, sucking on a pacifier, arms lifted and waiting for her to provide the expected comfort and shelter.

Nina lifted Holden in her arms, trying to ignore

the line of his nose and the slant of his forehead that with each passing day made him look more like his father. She held him tight, taking more time than she should to press his warm little body against hers, drawing in more comfort than she thought she could possibly be giving.

There was a pang of guilt about this—the notion that perhaps she was being selfish. But that couldn't be right, as the dull ache in her jaw reminded her.

Nina knew Holden wanted to eat, to suckle at her breast. If she did that now, though, this window of time could vanish. And so she promised to change his diaper and feed him at the first opportunity when she felt they were far enough.

Quicker now, she padded down the hall. The shadows leered at her, judges in the night. Nina heard a groan from their room, in their marriage bed. John always had a sixth sense, somehow knowing things before she knew them about herself, seeing in her things, terrible things.

She'd gotten the suitcases, one in each hand with her son in the crook of her arm. Nina teased open the front screen door with her elbow, pushed it forward with her knee, and braced her back against it. She held her foot out so as not to let it slam.

"*Dammit—*" she hissed, before clamping her mouth shut.

The keys were on the table.

Nina went back inside, leaned down, and picked up the keys with her teeth. She couldn't carry more if she tried. Yet she reminded herself that all mothers think this, and yet, somehow, they bear the weight.

Her son lifted his head from her shoulder and looked her in the eye. His mouth opened wide, dropping at the side, and he wailed. Fat tears spilled from the corners of his eyes. Nina followed his gaze back down that dark-shrouded hall.

And then she saw it.

The silhouette, the outline of the one thing that she forgot. Such an innocuous item of such importance—the lone, stuffed Stegosaurus, with its plate-like frill down its back.

If she didn't get it now, she'd never hear the end of it. She'd never be rid of the guilt of the one thing she left behind, the one comfort her sweet son clung to when he couldn't cling to her.

Nina set down the suitcases. Bile burned at the back of her throat. Of the tears trickling on her clavicle, she couldn't tell which belonged to her and which belonged to Holden.

Nina whispered sweet things to him—promises she wasn't sure she could keep, that she'd get the Stego for him. Each step she took felt like walking backward, further into the gloom where the light of the moon couldn't penetrate the shadows reaching to hold her down.

Faster than she dared, she bent and picked up the stuffed dinosaur. The blood in her veins turned to ice when, from the other side of the door, she heard a grumble and that word, that one, sickly sweet word.

"Honey?"

Nina had to say something. She *had* to keep it out of her voice.

"It's just Holden, sweetheart. I'm just gonna feed him real quick and put him down, okay? Don't you worry."

Don't you worry? What was she thinking? He was going to know.

The seconds between her heartbeats were an eternity.

"Okay. Come back to bed soon," he said.

She waited.

Finally, she heard another grumble, the tossing sheet, and whine of the bedsprings. Soft snores resumed. He'd just turned over.

She could've collapsed where she stood, planted in the hall, yet she found the will to gather all her items and leave, again.

With no incident, Nina loaded Holden into his car seat. It amazed her he didn't fuss. Her son was so tired—his eyelids drooped heavily as he looked at her balefully from out of the corner of them. She nestled Stego into his tiny, chubby arms. He clutched it tightly, closed his eyes, and succumbed to sleep.

All was quiet again.

She hadn't realized how loud her heart thundered in her ears. Nina got into the car and pulled out of the driveway, careful not to turn on the lights until she was down the street. Townhouses stood like faceless giants lining her way.

As she paused at the stop sign at the end of their road, brake lights came alive like red eyes against the rear windshield. She made a meager attempt to relax the tension, pinching her shoulders and unclenching her jaw.

"Nina!"

The sound of her name on the night air carried away all oxygen and left Nina clutching her chest. A dark silhouette closed in on her in the rearview mirror, marred by remnants of rain that glittered like drops of blood.

John.

Her heart raced. Nina gripped the wheel so hard her knuckles shone white and slammed her foot on the gas. From his rage-filled voice, she knew, without a doubt, that if he caught her, she was as good as dead.

2

Concrete and crowded houses gave way to a sprawling expanse of lush evergreen trees. Nina's car hungrily consumed the road. Night retreated against the slow rising light across the horizon, leaving long shadows across the landscape.

Nina ran her fingers through her hair, damp from sweat and stress, then dug into the glove compartment for a tissue. She blew her nose as quietly as she could. Holden was still sleeping in the back, and she didn't know how he'd managed not to wake with the *thump, thump, thump* of the balding tires over the unkempt New York back roads.

She patted her pocket, where the crinkle of a folded piece of paper, secreted away and protected for weeks from John's prying eyes, provided small comfort. On it, she could picture the scrawl of her own handwriting—the address of an old friend from high school. She and Bobbi hadn't talked in damn near a decade, but she prayed that what she recalled as a warm friendship could be rekindled. At least until Nina could get on her feet and support herself and Holden.

Nina's mouth went dry. Her heart quivered in

her chest at the thought of showing up on Bobbi's doorstep, unannounced and uninvited. This was intentional, though. She needed someone John didn't know, someone—somewhere—he wouldn't guess.

Truth was, Nina had done this before. Twice, even. Each time, he'd used his work connections and resources, not to mention his charming facade, to track her down. Nina's eyes welled. She couldn't even call her own mother.

She thought of her phone, its battery draining right where she'd left it, unplugged on her nightstand. Nina had learned the hard way that John could use it to locate her. Her credit cards, too, hadn't made her packing list. This time, she was running on the fumes of blind luck to survive. Nina looked in the mirror at Holden's peaceful face while he slept, then gripped the wheel harder and leaned on the accelerator.

Five towns over. That's all she needed to do—focus on the first step and trust that she would get through the next, and the next. She'd squirreled away as much cash as she could, but it would take a lot more to allow her to hop another few states away and start anew. She'd need to find a job as soon as possible.

Nina sniffled. She squinted down the road, trying to ignore a rising need to look over her shoulder. It wouldn't be long before she'd be forced to find a place to stop, and that sent fear bolting through her. Holden would need a change of diaper, to eat. She hoped she brought enough diapers to carry them through for a while. Diapers were a huge expense, and stretching her small wad of cash was going to be difficult.

The panels of the car seemed to press in too

close, her seat belt seeming to tighten across her chest and throat. She nearly choked on the cigarette smell that John's smoking had baked into the upholstery. Nina cranked down the window, rotating the manual handle in the aging vehicle.

Cool, crisp, early morning air swept over her, refreshing against her skin. Nina drew a haggard breath as if breathing for the first time. She dared a glint of hope—considered that, deep down, she'd never actually expected to succeed in her escape.

Ahead, a faded, peeling signpost came into view, advertising an off-the-beaten-path town coming up about a mile on her right. Nina could barely make out the name of the place. She leaned closer to the windshield, her headlights flashing over the cracked cursive lettering above the image of a gnarled apple tree:

Orchard Hill.

A black mass shot into the air and clouded the front of the car. Nina yelped as a hail-like noise pattered down around her in tiny metal *thunks*. Her vision became all but non-existent. Holden cried, near-screaming.

Nina jerked the wheel on reflex. Before she could regain control of herself and the vehicle, something that felt like a needle pierced her forearm, down to the bone, down to the marrow. She shrieked and swatted her arm in panic.

With no idea where the car was hurtling under this blinding black curtain, Nina rammed her foot, searching for the brake. In her hysteria, she accidentally slammed the accelerator, and the car lurched forward and the black mass on the windshield cleared, blowing away like dust in the wind. She smashed into the sign for Orchard Hill, wood chunks striking the car's glass, spawning spiderweb cracks.

Nina threw herself to the left, covering as much of the open driver's side window as she could to protect Holden while simultaneously toeing for the brake. It was impossible to do both at once, though, and as soon as the car was through the sign, they slammed to a stop. As her head whipped forward, Nina had the vague impression it was a tree they'd hit.

The car horn bleated in chorus with Holden's sobs. Stars burst before Nina's eyes. She clung to consciousness by embracing the pain of fresh injury. She repeatedly jerked against the tightened seat belt in an attempt to tend to the screaming child behind her, then calmed enough to jam her thumb into the seat belt button and free herself.

She scrambled onto the back seat, where she ran her hands all over his little body to make sure he was okay. Holden's tiny, chubby hands reached down. Nina looked to see Stego on the floorboards. She grabbed the plush dinosaur, brushed off dull flecks of glass, and released Holden from the car seat. He molded his body to her, holding tight to the stuffed animal and her shoulder.

When Holden's cries subsided, Nina pushed open the back door and got out to assess the damage. The entire front end of the car was crumpled, wrapped around the trunk of an old, decaying pine tree. Sliding into the front seat, she revved the engine to see if she could reverse the vehicle and at least limp along somewhere to get help.

The car was completely dead.

As Nina withdrew from the vehicle to gauge her limited options, she noticed something bright yellow and black on the floorboards. She leaned over to inspect it—a dead honeybee. She shifted Holden to her hip, recalling the stinging during the accident.

The black mass wasn't some malicious thing sent by her husband to stop her, to punish her. No, it had been nothing but a swarm of bees.

Cursing her terrible luck and not knowing what else to do—no phone, no nothing—Nina prayed her body had the endurance to do what she needed to do next. She opened the trunk, grabbed the two suitcases, chiding herself for thinking she'd packed light.

As she struggled down the road, juggling baby, bruises, and luggage, Nina hoped that the exit for Orchard Hill really was only a mile away, if she recalled correctly from the signpost she'd destroyed.

3

It couldn't have been much more than an hour, at least by Nina's estimation of the sunrise. Yet if she told time by the ache in her joints, or the sweat gathered in the pits of her arms, it felt far longer.

At last she reached what looked to be a general store. A single, ratty white pickup truck was parked in front. Dim lights inside shone through grimy windows plastered with retail stickers. It stood like a beacon off the isolated road, but Nina wasn't sure whether it was one of rescue or despair.

Behind the counter, she could make out a young man flipping through his phone, a trucker's hat pulled low over his eyes, his shoulders slouched. Holden was nuzzled against her, calm again, perhaps even sleeping. Nina nudged the door with her elbow to enter the tiny off-road mart. But of course, it was a pull, not push.

She tried subtly tapping on the thick panes to get the boy's attention, to no avail. Nina bit her bottom lip and released her luggage on the sidewalk, next to little tufts of grass poking through the cracked concrete. The air smelled earthier out here. She almost let herself enjoy it, before scanning the desolate parking lot for signs of other pa-trons, or—

Nina shook her head, refusing to follow her train of thought, and yanked on the store door. No one was going to take her luggage in the middle of nowhere.

The bell chimed as she entered, carrying Holden and searching for signs of the bathroom. She ex-pected the kid behind the counter would at least look up, if not exchange a pleasant enough greeting to calm her nerves. He didn't.

She shuffled to the bathroom in the back corner of the store, passing several rows stocked with dust-coated goods, more off brand than not. Under a flickering light, Nina cringed at the sticky changing station and cleaned what she could with a wipe be-fore laying her son on the tray table. Holden blinked up at her and squealed in delight before trying to wriggle away while she changed his dirty diaper.

Nina resorted to holding his hips down so she could get the new diaper secured. No leaks—good. Nina didn't know if she had the energy to battle with him to change his onesie and shorts. She managed to relieve herself and was washing her hands in the sink when she noticed herself in the mirror.

Her bruises had deepened into navy blues and sickly yellows. A bump on her forehead from hitting the steering wheel was a fine accessory to her swollen eye and jaw, giving her a gruff, angry look. It stung to look at, and her eyes welled. No makeup was up to the task of concealing her wounds, even if she had any on her. She slammed her fist against the mirror, holding back the full force of her fury and only rattling the glass. Holden laughed, and she snuggled him tight.

Emerging into the store, Nina pretended to browse the shelves and stole glances at the attendant to gauge his potential helpfulness. She wasn't optimistic. She also wasn't sure she had any other choice.

Walking up to the counter, Nina muttered a hello to the boy. Holden wriggled in her arms to be put down. The store wasn't large, maybe fifteen by fifteen feet, and she could see most of it from where she stood. Letting Holden wander a bit and stretch his legs in the confined space wasn't the worst idea. She knew if she didn't give him a chance to burn off some energy that she was going to have a very cranky baby on her hands—the last thing she needed.

Nina reluctantly set Holden down, keeping one eye on him as she again addressed the clerk. "Hello?" she waved a hand toward him. "Excuse me?"

He made an exasperated show of setting down his phone before coming over to the counter's edge. She swore he rolled his eyes, but it was hard to tell under the shadow of his cap. Acne scars marred his cheeks like freckles. He was older than she originally estimated.

"Yes, ma'am?" he said with a deadpan look and a small dose of upstate New York drawl.

"Yes, my car broke down. I mean, we were in an accident." Nina wiped her hand across her forehead and leaned over to check on Holden as he played with a bag of chips, enjoying the crinkling noise it made.

"You want me to call Triple A?" he asked.

"Uh, no." She felt a flush creep up her neck, with how limited her options were. "You see, the thing is . . . my circumstances are complicated."

His eyes roved over her bruises. The young man's apathetic assessment made Nina feel naked and vulnerable as if he looked right through her, her child, and her wounds, and couldn't muster up enough emotions to care.

Her mouth grew dry, and when she found the words for what kind of help she was asking for, she knew it was a long stretch. Nina cleared her throat. "Do you know where I might buy a car? The cheaper, the better."

The attendant raised an eyebrow, leaned back, and rubbed his chin. "Buy a new car? Here? Not really, ma'am. The only car I know of for sale 'round here is Jim Hayne's broken-down Mustang he's been trying to sell going on almost five years now. But something tells me even if you could afford it, you wouldn't want it."

Nina clenched her jaw and immediately regretted it, tentacles of pain clutching her face. She licked her lips and tried not to roll her eyes at the unhelpful man-child. "Okay . . . then do you know where I might find some work nearby?"

The young man, whose name, she saw from his crooked nametag, was Alan, scratched his head and fell quiet.

How could she get this far, and allow herself to be at the mercy of this clueless stranger?

As she sometimes did in her darkest moments, she imagined her life as a grave, and she lay at the bottom of it. Each time she tried to dig herself out, more dirt would be thrown on her than she could remove. Or it would rain so that every time she attempted to crawl out, to find some purchase, she'd slide right back in. With only a couple hundred bucks to her name, two suitcases—mostly full of diapers and wipes—and her son, what hope did she have to get them away from John for good?

Nina perked up. Where was Holden? She looked —then heard happy mumbling coming from nearby. He'd found something to chew on.

Disregarding Alan's beginning attempt at a paltry reply, Nina raced around the shelves, praying that whatever Holden had gotten hold of wasn't toxic or a choking hazard. As she scooted around the corner, Nina noticed two vehicles now in the lot.

Her heart thumped, stronger. Tears burned her eyes, and she started rehearsing her pleas for mercy, hoping that John would only direct his fury at her and not Holden.

Nina stopped dead in her tracks when she looked down the aisle. When she didn't see any sign of John, her body heaved a sigh of relief.

Yet Holden was not alone.

Hovering over her son was a skeleton of a woman—tall, in her eighties at least, with a remark-able bone structure that gave her cheekbones a ra-zor's edge. She wore high-waisted black trousers and a black blouse with three-quarter sleeves. Her white and dark gray hair was French braided to the nape of her neck, in striking, alternating stripes.

The woman held something out to Holden. Nina couldn't see what it was, but Holden appeared to be sucking on it. Puffing back up, Nina charged forward.

"Get away from my son!" She snatched Holden up in her arms and yanked whatever it was out of his mouth.

It surprised Nina when the old woman rose gracefully to an erect posture, not crouched with age in the least, nor startled by Nina's ferocity. A good foot taller than Nina—her presence was imposing. It didn't matter, though: Nina's instincts were in overdrive.

With a wry smile, the woman said, "Why, it's just a bit of honey, child." She presented the half-eaten tiny plastic tube, and Holden reached for it.

"Why are you giving my son anything?" Nina said. "He's not even quite a year yet. You can't give him honey."

"What do you mean? Children love honey. It makes sure that they will grow up kind and sweet." The old woman held her fingers in a down-pointed steeple, clearly unperturbed by Nina's anger.

Nina hated getting advice from other women on motherhood, especially ones who were mothers themselves and, even more so, those for whom several decades had passed since their children were babies. She sighed.

"Pediatricians don't recommend honey for children under one year old."

The woman pointed a crooked finger toward Holden. Nina saw she hadn't entirely escaped the ravages of age as it had hit the old woman in her gnarled hands. "That boy can't be less than a year's old. Look at him—he's been toddling around like a little giant in this store."

Nina's nostrils flared. "He's on the big end of the chart for his age, yes. His . . . father is big too. A lot of the people in my family are a good foot taller than me. He was always going to be big." Nina switched Holden to her opposite hip, suddenly aware of how heavy he was. "It doesn't matter, though. You shouldn't be feeding someone else's child."

The old woman dipped her head at Nina with the grace of a queen. Now that she was closer, Nina

saw that the woman wore yellow eyeshadow, like
smears of pollen over her eyelids. Her lips were no-
ticeably red. She couldn't help thinking the woman
must have been quite the head-turner when she was
younger, if this was how she looked in her winter
years.

"I offer my apologies." The woman pressed her
steepled fingers to her lips, then pointed them again
at Holden. "The child seemed hungry."

Nina didn't think it was fair to interpret her
statement as judgmental, but still, guilt tugged at
her. It was way past the time to breastfeed Holden,
and the weight of her breasts, full to bursting,
agreed. She needed to feed her son very soon, not
just for his sake, but for hers as well.

A measure of silence passed between the women
—the older woman appeared completely at peace
with it, while Nina hummed with anxiety.

"All right then." The woman squeezed Nina's
arm. Then, with measured steps, she walked to the
counter with her small basketful of items and
checked out. As she left, she turned back to Nina
and raised a precipitous eyebrow. "I heard you were
asking for work?"

Nina wanted to drop to her knees. If she was
going to keep Holden and herself safe, she needed
to get used to relying on the kindness of strangers. It
left a bitter taste in her mouth. Nina looked down at
Holden and back to the woman. She opened her
mouth, then settled on just a nod. Why was this
woman throwing her a bone?

Without a word, the old woman walked outside,
the door chiming. She deftly picked up Nina's two
suitcases and headed toward a dark gray pickup.

Did she really agree to go with this strange

woman? Tightness gripped her chest like a vise. She didn't have Bobbi's phone number, and her address was too far away to ask for a ride. If this allowed her to make enough cash to travel the rest of the way, it seemed like her best shot. She took several deep breaths and headed for the door with Holden.

Nina swore the attendant shook his head disapprovingly as she passed him. But she ignored him and hurried outside just as the old woman placed the suitcases into the cargo bed of her truck and closed the tailgate.

"Wait!" Nina called out to her. "What kind of work do you have?"

The old woman cocked her head in a sidelong glance. "I need an extra pair of hands around my orchard. Someone to help tend to the house." She gestured to the passenger side and got behind the wheel.

Nina hesitated, then reasoned it was risky to stick around the general store much longer. She slid into the passenger seat, careful not to bump Holden's head and hating that she'd have to hold him in her lap while they drove. It wasn't safe. A small voice inside her answered, *nothing is safe.* She refused to accept that.

Sitting so close to the old woman, her regal presence and sweet perfume unavoidable, Nina realized she didn't even know her name. Silently, Nina cursed John for putting her in a situation where she felt she had no other option than to get into a stranger's car.

"Excuse me, ma'am," Nina said, stinging herself with the extra politeness in her tone, "but did you tell me your name?"

"Greta." She offered Nina her hand. "My name is Greta."

Nina took it. "Nina. And this here's Holden."

Greta disengaged the parking brake and started to pull out when an open-palmed hand slapped the passenger's side window, startling Nina and Holden. She expected to see John, the jig up before it began. For as long as she could remember, Nina felt there was a long, unseen, unbreakable tether between them.

Slowly, Nina turned her head, sensing the male presence, savoring every moment she had left. When she saw Alan, the attendant, Nina rubbed her lips together in a tight line, then comforted her son by stroking his cheek.

Alan tapped the glass again until Nina rolled down the window.

"Yes, Alan?" she said, through clenched teeth.

He lifted his hat and scratched his head, where a surprisingly bright ginger tuft grew. "I just remembered, ma'am. There's a car dealership about five miles up the road. Maybe they could help you."

Whereas before his eyes had been diluted, now they were wide with fear. His pupils like pinpoints, Alan looked at Nina, the ground, everything to seemingly avoid looking at Greta beside her.

Nina considered that she should get out of the car and try taking Alan's advice. It was the first time he'd actually tried to help her. She glanced at the dashboard clock, its weak blue light showing six o'clock in the morning. Had it truly been so long since she'd left the house?

Her eyes screamed for sleep. Nina cracked open the truck's door an inch, thinking to chat with Alan a bit longer, to ask Greta to wait a minute while she figured out what to do.

Two yellow eyes rose in the distance on the road, beams of light from a turning vehicle.

Alan whistled.

"My goodness, so many visitors today. Hardly anyone comes out this way. Except on occasion—" He gestured with his chin at Greta. "Wonder who it could be?"

Nina's stomach sank. She knew exactly who it could be. Despite Alan's resistance, Nina yanked the door shut and turned to Greta. "Let's go."

With an equally stern nod, Greta pulled out of the parking lot. Nina scooted down in the seat, softly singing a lullaby to Holden. She didn't dare glance in the rearview mirror.

4

Nina crouched in the car seat, cradling Holden as Greta drove, stiff-backed and shoulder-straight, away from the general store. She felt ridiculous. There was no way her husband knew which way she was going now. She was being paranoid. Those headlights certainly weren't him.

Holden nuzzled her breast, searching for milk. "Mind if I . . .?" Nina asked.

Greta arched her brow, but simply nodded.

Nina unbuttoned her shirt with one hand, and Holden soon found what he was looking for and began suckling. The farther they drove, the harder it was for Nina to think of something to say. It wasn't often that she spoke with someone outside the small circle of police officers' wives.

Nina cleared her throat and swallowed.

"Married?" That single word from Greta's lips held decades of sentiment, though Nina couldn't discern the woman's exact feelings on the matter.

"Yes, ma'am."

"How long?" Greta asked.

Nina did a quick tally in her head. "It'll be four years this March."

Saying it out loud, Nina wondered where those years had gone. They were a smear of meals served to John, which, after she got pregnant, became a smear of sleepless nights. She vaguely recalled being happy once. Early on. But now, the only warmth she felt in her heart was when her son smiled at her and giggled.

Timid young sunlight shone across the sky. Holden peeked up at her from her breast and issued a small grin. Nina smiled, a genuine thing, and rubbed his back. Then she deftly switched him to the other side.

"What kind of orchard is it . . . or farm?" Nina asked.

"It's an apple orchard. Though it's been some time since it operated as a regularly running orchard with an open-picking season. They're hardy things, though. They just keep on blooming each year." Greta cocked her head at Nina and smiled. Her teeth were emaciated yellowing pillars in her mouth, an odd contrast to her lipstick.

Nina hoped her own smile didn't look as uncomfortable as it felt.

"The real pride of the orchard are my honeybees," Greta said.

How far out was this orchard? The clock informed Nina they'd been driving for nearly twenty minutes. She tried to ignore the creeping sensation up her back that she'd made the wrong choice.

"Honeybees?" Without meaning to, Nina ran her hand along the angry bump on her arm.

Greta's eyes darted to the welt. Nina had a feeling that no detail went unnoticed by this woman. "Not fond of the creatures?"

Greta's slender fingers gripped the steering

wheel tighter as they took a left turn down a narrow lane. The trees curled over them, forming a small dark tunnel.

"Why would I be fond of them? They're annoying bugs that sting you. I'm pretty sure that's what caused my . . ." Nina wasn't sure she should tell Greta about her car accident. She wasn't sure why. Would Greta make her call the cops? Still, the fewer details, the better.

Greta's jaw flexed and nostrils flared. "I understand that's a common feeling about bugs. Insects. However, without bees we'd all be dead."

Expecting the lecture to continue, Nina longed to scratch the rising itch between her shoulder blades. The word *dead* reverberated in the truck's cabin, and Nina hurried to replace the lull with any other sound. "I'm sorry ma'am. I didn't mean to offend. Most of my life, I've only ever lived in the suburbs, so I don't really know much about country life."

This caused Greta to chuckle. Nina allowed her own shoulders to relax. She cuddled with Holden, who had fallen asleep.

"That's okay," Greta said. "You'll have plenty of opportunity to learn more about them at Orchard Hill."

"Speaking of, when do you think we'll get there?"

The trees' hovering clawed hands spread, reaching, almost praying. Hills opened up on either side of the road, where shorter trees stood like rows and rows of hunchbacks in the dawning light.

"We're here now. The house is just up at the top of the hill."

They drove up the incline. Apple trees stretched

as far as the eye could see, and Nina grew very aware of how far away they were from the general store, let alone any main throughway roads. She didn't even know which direction the town was in, or how to get there. Without her own vehicle, she'd be at Greta's whims, and while Greta seemed nice, she also appeared to have a stern personality, with unknown moods that could easily be triggered.

Nina gripped her son tighter to her chest and said a silent prayer. As they crested the hill, the truck groaned. The quality of the road deteriorated the closer they got to the house. Greta cranked the parking brake, and the pickup lurched to a stop.

Holden stirred from his slumber. A stench filled the car.

"I need to change his diaper," Nina said.

Nina's hand was already on the door handle, opening the door. Greta wrapped her iron grip around Nina's wrist, which demanded Nina stop and look her in the eye. "Orchard Hill is my home. While you're here, working for me, you will respect me, this house, my rules, and the bees."

Nina was sure her own eyes had bugged out of her head. She wanted nothing more than to tend to her son and ignore the potential crazy brewing in this woman in front of her.

"Greta, I don't mean any harm. I'll do as you say. I just need a place for me and my son until I can get back on my feet. Then we'll be out of your hair. I promise you won't even notice we're here."

Greta's cold eyes narrowed at Nina, her red lips taut. Then the look melted, replaced with a serene smile. Greta laughed. "Don't look so frightened, child. I meant what I said, but no need to worry. I think you'll do just fine here."

Greta released her iron hold and patted Nina right on her bee sting. Nina did her best not to flinch at the dull pain that ensued. With one last glance at Greta, Nina slipped out of the vehicle.

Before retrieving her items from the trunk, Nina couldn't help but stare at the farmhouse in front of her. Painted a fading, pollen-yellow, its face was covered in shadow. Shutters stood askance, and several panes were broken, like cracked open eyelids. There were three floors, it looked like, and a wraparound porch. The whole thing could well have been over a hundred years old. The hair on the back of her neck rose, and she shivered.

Nina adjusted Holden higher on her shoulder as she plucked her bags from the back of the pickup. Greta had already grabbed one of them and was marching up the creaking stairs to the front door. Nina reluctantly followed.

The door looked freshly painted in contrast to the peeling yellow siding. It was solid oak coated in a dark black. Nina juggled her son and items while waiting for Greta to insert a heavy, ornate, gold key into an equally cumbersome lock.

The inside of the house was draped in darkness, the air sickly sweet and stale. None of this surprised Nina. Older women's homes tended to smell like layers upon layers of perfume, candle scents, and potpourri. This might be an attempt on Greta's part to cover up the smells of age and looming death. Nina shook her head to wipe away the morbid thoughts. If anything, Greta was in better shape than she was.

Nina expected Greta to flip on the lights, but instead was led deeper into the cocooning darkness.

She flinched when Greta yanked a lightbulb chain and illuminated the bathroom.

Greta held the door open and stood aside. "Will this do for now?"

Nina nodded her thank you and ducked inside with Holden. As she crouched on the floor, her knees against the old bubble tile, she engaged in the brief struggle with her son to change his diaper without getting its contents all over the floor.

The diaper change completed, Nina let her son toddle around the enclosed space, under her supervision. "What do you think, honey bunny? Will this do for now?"

Holden looked up at her, uncharacteristically quiet. No babbling for today.

Nina reached to turn the iron faucet handle set in the stained porcelain sink. The rim of the sink was decorated in hand-painted blue and pink flowers, along which she ran her fingertips. They lay beneath a worn coat of gloss that warped the pretty petals. When she turned the handle, the pipes whined so loudly she jumped and yelped.

From the other side of the door, Greta hollered, "Try the left one!"

Nina licked her lips, holding her hand to her chest. She turned off the right handle and turned on the left. Brown water spurted out at her, until it finally ran clear and cool from the faucet.

As Nina washed her hands, Greta offered, "We run on well water here. Sometimes the pipes get fussy about it."

Drying her hands on the hand towel (not hardly big enough for its purpose), Nina glanced down to check on Holden. He had gotten hold of a candle and had begun gnawing on it. Nina cursed herself for such carelessness and kneeled to take the item from her son.

With her finger, she cleaned out his mouth. It didn't seem like much actually got in, just a few waxy shavings. Holden pouted and reached for the candle as she inspected it.

Wound in intricate spirals, the candle appeared to be made of raw beeswax, visible honeycombs and all. A wick jutted from the middle as one would expect. But when Nina looked at the milky white and yellow sides, she swore there were specks of . . . something . . . deeper within.

She brought the candle closer, holding her breath and peering at one speck in particular: dark, almost the size of her pinky nail. The world receded for a moment.

By some trick of the eye, the speck moved.

She waited.

It twitched. Yes, it *twitched*. Her heart palpitated.

Greta banged on the door, and Nina dropped the candle. Holden crouched to retrieve his prize, now rolling on the floor. Bile rose in Nina's throat as she retrieved the candle and replaced it on the dusty shelving.

Nina scooped up Holden, took a shuddering breath, and opened the door.

5

Nina emerged from the tiny bathroom, half-expecting Greta to be standing there, sternly waiting. Yet the foyer was empty, the only company a parade of dust motes floating in the early morning light.

Uneasiness crawled up Nina's back, worked down, and numbed her fingers. A low static hum filled the air. The place was alternately discomforting and comforting, a heavy blanket weighing her down.

Awaiting Greta's return, Nina shifted Holden's weight from one side to another on her hip. She ran her fingers along the entry table that overflowed with keys, buttons, and other choking-hazard trinkets. She withdrew her fingers as they came away with a sticky residue—a soft, hard-to-scrub dust accumulated over many years.

"Greta?" Nina ventured, her heartbeat speeding up.

She meandered over to the front door windows. Brushing away with her wrist some of the cloudy buildup on the glass, she squinted. Orchard Hill farmhouse rested atop the highest hill and afforded clear views over the rolling landscape. There were no lights from any towns, or from the general store, just miles of squat apple trees, and, where those ended, a line of taller forest pines encompassing the orchard.

Nina hugged Holden tighter to her. While nothing could make her return to that house with John, she wasn't sure this place was safe, either. Despite the expansiveness of nature outside, the isolation was palpable.

A floorboard creaked behind her, and Nina jumped.

A sharp *crack*, then a *buzz* and *pop*. This time, Nina didn't jump, yet she was unable to suppress a twitch in her shoulder at the noise.

"Greta?" Nina called.

"I'm in here, child." The word *child* again grated on Nina's ears, and she swore there was a hint of impatience in the old woman's tone.

Making her way deeper into the house, Nina walked slowly at first, then picked up her pace. The hall was cast in such a heavy darkness that it gave her brief flashbacks to her own hallway that she nearly didn't escape from.

She reached a swinging door, listened to the sounds coming from the other side. Sizzling, followed by scraping. Seconds after, the smell reached her, and her stomach rumbled.

The swinging door squealed on its hinges as Nina and Holden entered the large kitchen. The appliances were heavy and caked with age and years of use. A broad, eastern-facing window sat over a deep sink, allowing in cheerful sunlight. The sun brightened over the horizon, the golden hue bringing a warm glow to the timeworn kitchen.

Greta carried an antique—perhaps multi-generational—cast-iron skillet and slipped some eggs, sunny side up, onto a plate. She slid the plate over the kitchen island toward Nina, who took a seat on one of the wooden high-back chairs. Nina opened her mouth to comment on the yolks, but Greta halted her with one raised finger.

The old woman swiveled about, returning with what looked like one egg's worth of scrambled eggs. "I know, I know. He can't have raw yoke."

Nina offered a small, uncomfortable smile. "Thank you, ma'am."

Greta nodded. "You're welcome, my dear."

Nina didn't waste time scarfing down her eggs. All the stress of the past evening and morning left her hungrier than she'd time to acknowledge. With a loud exclamation, Holden echoed her sentiments. Nina shoveled eggs into his mouth while she finished her meal.

Greta washed up, dishes clanging lightly, not turning around. On her last bite, Nina choked on a bit of the egg and coughed. Before she could make the request for water, Greta was filling a glass from the tap and setting it before her.

Nina gulped down the cool liquid, noting a metallic taste. It wasn't bad. Just different.

"Thank you."

Greta leaned forward on sharp elbows and propped herself on the kitchen island. She didn't reply. Instead, she looked down her long, aquiline nose, studying Nina.

Holden cooed for more food, and Nina offered another spoonful of eggs, which he gobbled up. Greta smiled warmly at him and, while at some level it softened Nina toward her, on another, it added to the unease. Nina tried to tell herself it made sense that Greta would have much less judgment for a baby than for her.

After several moments of uncomfortable silence, Greta spoke.

"Clearly you're running from something, girl. I can just about guess what. I don't want any trouble at my orchard, as you well know. But having been a mother myself, I can tell when another mother is in need, and I'm not one to cast her out." Greta's steely eyes offered nothing of the emotions behind her words. "Tend to the house and the orchard, as I instruct. I'll give you room and board, including food, which you'll have to help cook, of course. I'll pay three hundred a week. You can stay here as long as you like until you're ready to get back on your feet and move on."

Greta wiped her hand on her apron, extended it to Nina, and added, "We have a deal?"

6

Nina froze. She knew this was exactly the offer she needed, exactly when she needed it most. Greta, though off-putting, seemed genuine enough. Yet the prospect of staying in and caring for this hulking, shadowy farmhouse made her stomach churn.

An anxious squeal from Holden snapped her out of it, and Nina struggled to get the words out. "Can I think about it?"

Greta eyed Nina with a skeptical look. Then the older woman retreated from the kitchen island and issued a curt nod.

In Nina's lap, Holden had finished downing his eggs and was rubbing his eyes.

"It's about time for his nap. Do you have a place where I might put him down?" Nina asked.

Greta pressed a long nail to her red lips as she grew pensive. "You know, I just might. In the attic."

The notion of an attic in this place sent more shivers down Nina's back. She followed Greta out of the kitchen and up a narrow flight of creaky stairs. Nina pictured a cramped, mote-filled tomb matching the outdated farmhouse apple decor she'd already seen in the foyer and kitchen.

As Nina struggled to keep Holden in her arms while they marched up a flight of steps to the first landing, Greta required the aid of the banisters a tad more than Nina had expected. The shield on Nina's heart lowered a little. Did Greta need her help just as much as Nina needed hers?

Only able to glimpse a long hallway with three or four doors on each side of the first floor, the trio traipsed up to the second level. As anticipated, this floor had fewer rooms. The house was wider at its base and tapered off to the pinnacle of the roof.

Two doors were closed on the second floor, and Nina wondered what lay behind them. Alan's words of caution echoed back to her. Nina knew small towns had a way of vilifying older women, especially those living alone. The town she'd grown up in was small enough to have an old "witch" of its own. But Ms. Keeler wouldn't hurt a fly. Not that Nina as a child believed that . . . until one day, when she was twelve, her father, who ran the local grocery, sent her on a mission to deliver some cat food and milk to Ms. Keeler. Nina still remembered the fear of going up the "thorn witch's" walk, overgrown rose bushes leering at her from their untrimmed hedges.

Yet Nina's father had said to mind her manners. Being given the rare opportunity to make him proud, Nina wasn't going to let him down. When Ms. Keeler bade Nina inside, Nina didn't flinch. She entered, head held high and arms full of groceries, and, wouldn't you know, Ms. Keeler wasn't scary at all. The "witch" turned out to be a lonely old woman, whose kids and grandkids lived too far away to visit often. She'd served Nina warm snickerdoodle cookies and even let her pet her Maine coon, Hank, the biggest, softest cat Nina had ever encountered. Nina wouldn't ever forget that day.

Though Greta's attitude and farmhouse were night and day from Ms. Keeler's, Nina wasn't keen on buying into the rumors of intrigue that so often spread like wildfire through the gossip network of a small town. Everyone's lens on life was so thoroughly shrouded in their own point of view, you could never guarantee any opinion was giving someone a fair shake. Why hadn't this prevented her from ending up with a man like John? Perhaps she kept expecting his better side to show. The more she dug, though, all she'd found was rot.

Nina felt a sleepy Holden nuzzle her shoulder. She ran her fingers over his soft, fine hair, and she melted. Despite the pain her marriage to John had brought, she could never regret the situation that bestowed such love in her life.

Greta cleared her throat, drawing Nina out of her thoughts. Leaning forward, she withdrew a slender brass key from her front pocket and unlocked the door at the top of the third-floor staircase. A stream of light poured through a murky porthole window in the door, catching on a necklace that slipped out of Greta's workman's blouse. Nina did her best to casually inspect the necklace without alerting Greta.

At the end of the delicate chain was a tiny glass vial, plugged with an ocher-colored wax stopper. Inside was a dried bee, its fluffy headdress a brilliant yellow. A nasty stinger protruded from its abdomen, heightening Nina's awareness of the small buzz of pain from the stinger that had found her skin earlier.

"That's an . . . interesting necklace?" Nina tried to hide the disgust from her voice.

Greta pushed open the attic door, which squealed on its rusty hinges. Nina imagined all hinges in this house wailed for some WD-40. Despite having not formally accepted Greta's offer, Nina was already making a mental checklist of tasks to hit first to get the house back into shape.

"Do you like it?" Greta asked, holding the vial up to the scant light. Nina swore there was a distant sadness in the woman's eyes. "This is a queen bee."

Nina had a hard time choosing one of the million questions she had about why Greta would want to wear a necklace with a dead bee in it, but that was soon replaced with the million questions she had about the contents of the attic.

The attic reminded Nina of a giant gazebo, or rotunda. Round glass windows ringing every wall, all grayed by layers of faded newspaper. Where the newspaper sagged, the glass's amber tint cast the room in a dim honeyed light. She imagined how stunning the room would be once she cleaned it up. The view of the orchard had to be spectacular.

Nina frowned, cradling Holden against her, wondering why Greta would keep such a room closed up and cloaked in darkness when it so clearly yearned for light.

She took a couple of tentative steps further into the attic and paused. The one detail her imagination had got right about the room was its plethora of forgotten boxes and furniture, most of which were covered with grimy yellowed sheets. Making her way further into the space, she brushed against a box and unleashed a cloud of dust.

Nina did her best to suppress a sneezing fit and

was pleased when Holden didn't stir from her shoulder. She expected a woman like Greta to be very vigilant about issuing *bless yous*. However, when Nina half-turned back to the door, Greta's eyes were downcast, and she wore a deeply lined frown.

Uncrossing her arms and looking up, Greta lifted a limp hand toward the center of the room. It was hard for Nina to discern whether the old woman's eyes watered from the dust or sadness.

Nina furrowed her eyebrows and was about to say something when Greta said, "Some of the old nursery furniture, including a crib, should be underneath the sheets right there. Why don't you hunt around for it while I pop down to the second-floor bath and grab you a rag to wipe it down?"

"Sure." Nina barely got any other word out before Greta trotted off downstairs. Nina listened to Greta's quickening footsteps and could have sworn the woman desired to be anyplace else. Had coming in the attic churned up old sorrows, alongside the dust?

Nina hoisted Holden a little higher on her shoulder and took a three-sixty scan of the room. "It really will be beautiful up here after a little cleaning," she whispered to her son.

He cooed a soft response. If she didn't hurry and lay him down somewhere safe, he was just going to finish out the whole nap on her shoulder. Not that she minded all that much, but the child was heavy for his age. Her back screamed with his weight, and the less-than-ideal nap could make for a cranky baby in the afternoon.

What time was it, anyhow? The covered windows offered little sunlight to hazard a guess. Maybe eleven, or noon. Her nose was stuffy, her allergies

agitated in the dust. She sniffled. Usually she didn't
react this way to average house dust, not that this
was average. It was more like her reaction to
summer pollen.

Her senses adjusting to the dimly lit attic, she
dragged a finger through the grime on one of the
nearby sheets. Her fingertip came away with a thick
layer, and there was indeed a dark yellow contained
within. Nina rubbed her forefinger and thumb,
feeling a hint of stickiness. She expected it nearer to
the kitchen, where grease might create that effect on
household surfaces. But here, all the way in the
attic? Odd.

Another oddity: the farmhouse never seemed
truly silent, or still. There was a subtle, unnerving
vibration to the place, detectable in every room.
Nina sniffled again and heard a similar sound
downstairs.

Was Greta crying?

Nina backpedaled toward the door, then
changed her mind. Someone like Greta would want
her privacy. At least, that's what Nina preferred
when she was upset.

Soon, Nina had wandered toward the middle of
the attic, exactly where Greta had directed her to go
in search of nursery furniture. The waist-high, rec-
tangular shape was probably the crib Greta had in-
dicated. The room was darkest here, the evidence of
untouched age the greatest.

Hiking Holden up higher on her shoulder, Nina
extended a trembling hand to the sheet. As she
grabbed a clump of fabric, her senses recoiled at the
inch of fluffy, sticky dust. It would take weeks for her
to clean up just this room. Buckets of soapy water.
Heaps of scrubbing.

Nina had drawn the sheet off halfway when she paused, cocking her head to the side. Noise caught in her ear like radio static on a dead channel. Something wasn't right.

She drew in a sharp breath and chuckled nervously. Greta was harmless, especially compared to what she was running from, and there was nothing up here in this old attic that was out to get her. Nina was just bone tired, frazzled, sorely in need of a good night's rest.

She tugged the sheet the rest of the way off and immediately shrank back, covering her mouth to stifle the scream.

Nestled inside the crib was a swarming nest of bees.

7

Nina struggled against the cobwebs of sleep. In the pitch-black room, she reached out for her phone on her nightstand to check the baby monitor, then sprung upright. Her hand plunged into emptiness—she wasn't home. She was at Orchard Hill.

The bed on which she rested was a twin bed, covered in a heavy quilt. Her eyes blinked, owl wide, trying to pick up on any light. Still navigating a thick haze of sleep, she remembered the moments before she found herself in Greta's guest bed.

Nina remembered slamming the attic door shut against the bees, the afterimage of the mass rising from the crib, a nightmare imprinted in her mind. She'd sprung out of the room with Holden and flung herself against the door. When she'd raced downstairs and told Greta about the bees' nest in the attic, the old woman only nodded like it came as no surprise to her.

Greta had led Nina and Holden to the guest room to rest, patting Nina on the arm all the while and assuring her that she'd take care of the bees, everything would be alright. Despite not being too keen on Holden sleeping out of the crib, Nina had snuggled him close. The hollowness of his absence blossomed with a sickly dread that started in her stomach and spread everywhere.

Nina hopped out of bed, searching her memory for the layout of the room. If she remembered correctly, there was a light switch to the right of the door, a few feet to her left. She spread her hands blindly in front of her and felt a small measure of relief when her palm caught the switch, and clicked on the overhead light.

She threw open the oak door and skidded into the hallway. With a quick glance left and right, she saw the spread of doors that meant she was on the first floor. When she'd laid down next to Holden to watch him while he napped, she'd curled her arm around him, fighting the heaviness of her own eyelids.

Cursing herself for falling asleep, she couldn't fathom how, even if he got off the bed, he would've gotten out of the room, especially when the door was still closed, and he wasn't quite tall enough to reach up and turn the knob. But if she'd learned anything about her growing boy, it was that he was always two steps ahead of where she thought he was.

"Holden?" she called down the hall, panic threatening to strangle her vocal cords.

Nina raced to the staircase landing, looked up and down, fretting. Her heart thundered in her chest, ready to break free. The edges of Nina's emotions unraveled with worry. Horrific possibilities of what had happened to her baby flashed through her mind. Falling down the stairs. Tangled in curtain cords. Choking on some small object, of which there were many in this house.

This house.

Geriatric houses, such as this Orchard Hill farm-house, always had a weightiness to their presence. At first, Nina cowered under its pressure as if it were watching her with heavy-lidded eyes, judging her every step. Before she became a mother herself, she had no concept of the precious burden mothers carried in their hearts. Not only was there the constant terror of losing one's child—there was truly the earth-shattering horror of not being able to live up to the role. Because in being a parent, letting your child down can mean life or death, and even if it doesn't mean death, one wrong misstep can leave a permanent imprint.

In the seconds that Nina stood frozen on the staircase, her posture had caved in on itself. From her shirt, she caught a whiff of her child's scent. This was all she needed. Nina shoved her shoulders back, lifted her head high, and tore down the stairs.

"Holden!" Her forceful voice carried on the ground floor, bouncing back to her, strengthening her confidence.

Nina paused, tense and poised to act. She strained for any sound of Holden.

Delighted giggling wafted from the kitchen, followed by Greta's voice. Simultaneous relief and fury flooded her veins. Nina did her best not to slam the swinging door open as she entered, but she did nothing to hold back the stomp of her feet as she approached her child and lifted him in her arms.

"Oh, heavens." Greta pressed a spindly hand to her own chest and showed genuine empathy. "You, poor dear, I'm so sorry. You must've had no idea where he'd gotten off to when you awoke. I heard him crying and figured he was hungry. You must've been so exhausted, you didn't even hear him, or me coming in to get him."

The sheer gall of this woman. Nothing in her would ever believe she'd sleep through her son's cries. Nina used to sleep like a rock before she had Holden. Yet since the day he was born, she'd awaken at the slightest sound he made, no matter how tired she was.

Clenching her teeth against the flurry of insults she wanted to hurl at Greta, Nina just smiled and nodded. It wouldn't do to piss Greta off over something like this. With as sweet a tone as she could muster, she said, "Next time, please wake me up?"

Greta handed Holden his stuffed stegosaurus. Nina wanted to scream at them—for Greta to keep her bony hands off her boy and his dinosaur, for Holden not to be so damn happy and smile at the old woman so.

He didn't know any better, though, and no harm had been done. As long as Holden was safe.

"Sure thing." Greta stood straight and waved a hand at the refrigerator. "Why don't I rustle up some supper for us and get you both back to bed? You can start in on cleaning the attic out tomorrow morning, after I transfer the bees to my hive."

They ate together in silence, punctuated only by the insistent screams from Holden for more food as the evening matured into night.

While Nina readied herself and Holden for bed, Greta appeared in the guest bedroom doorway. Outstretched in her arms were a couple of beige towels, what looked to be a brand-new toothbrush, and a set of lavender-colored linen pajamas. "Here you go. Goodnight."

Greta disappeared before Nina could offer a

heartfelt thank you. As Nina shut the bedroom door, she promised herself she'd attempt to be more grateful to this woman offering shelter in her time of need.

Nina crawled into bed with Holden, cuddling close with him. She left the nightstand lamp on, and barely remembered her head hitting the pillow.

The night passed without incident, except for one thing. At some point in the middle of the night, her eyes flew open. The lamp threw crooked shadows against the wallpaper patterned with green leaves and red apples.

She'd almost fallen back asleep when she heard a soft scratching sound that appeared to be coming from one of the interior walls. Not wanting to disturb Holden, who, uncharacteristically, appeared to be sleeping like an angel tonight, she couldn't get up to investigate and was forced to chalk it up to the groanings of an old house.

Nina let her eyes close. The sound followed her into her dreams, where she had a nightmare about the bees in the attic.

8

After freshening up herself and Holden and brushing their teeth, Nina emerged from the guest bath. She straightened at the *clomp clomp clomp* of steps down the staircase, followed by a loud buzzing.

From the flight of steps between the second and first floor, a hulking white figure, speckled black and yellow, moved methodically onto the landing. In its arms was an enormous white box, lid askew. Nina took two steps back and barricaded herself and a crying Holden in the bathroom. She really wished Greta would've given her a heads up about removing the bees—then she remembered Greta mentioning wanting to do it first thing in the morning. Still, Nina could've used a little advance notice.

Perspiration beaded her forehead. Was Holden allergic to bees? She didn't even know. That fear kept her and Holden in the bathroom longer than she cared to admit.

Eventually, though, Holden whined for breakfast, and she couldn't stay in the guest bath all day. Her own stomach rumbled in sympathy.

By the time she got to the kitchen, Greta already

had laid out a full spread of breakfast—bacon, eggs, bagels, and sliced fruit. Holden's eyes lit up at all the food, and Nina knew he would try to eat it all if she let him. Next to the kitchen island sat an antique high chair. Nina slipped Holden into it, and started putting together a plate for herself and Holden. It dawned on Nina that the box brimming with the bees' nest, and the high chair, couldn't have been easy to carry from the attic down three flights of stairs. Greta may not be as frail as she thought.

"Wow, did you get this all the way from the attic?" Nina asked.

Greta motioned for Nina to take the seat next to her, and didn't begin eating her food until Nina took a bite of hers. "I did, yes. But if you want anything else, you'll have to do it yourself. The bees are clear."

"Yes, I saw you coming down the stairs. Is that a special box for the bees?"

Greta arched her brows at Nina. "I didn't realize you were awake."

Greta was a woman of very little affect, yet Nina would've sworn that this news caught her off guard. Nina ruffled Holden's hair and put more fruit on his plate. "Oh, you know the little ones. They never let you sleep in."

"Yes, well, I never was one to sleep in myself, anyway. The day starts early when tending to an orchard and household."

Just when Nina thought she was making headway with the woman, Greta would say something that could be interpreted as judgment. Or perhaps Nina was just primed to be sensitive right now. Pushing away from the table, Nina picked up hers and Greta's empty plates.

"I'll get that, child." Greta motioned to a pair of gloves, a small pile of frayed rags, and a gray-and-white striped head scarf neatly folded on the counter. "Why don't you go ahead and get started upstairs in the attic? I'll clean up from breakfast and watch the little munchkin."

"Okay." Nina moved hesitantly toward the counter. "Please holler if he needs anything. I'll come right down."

Greta added more eggs to Holden's plate, and he bounced up and down with excitement. "Of course."

Nina kissed Holden on the forehead and took the cleaning items off the counter. She expected Holden to protest, but he seemed oddly at ease with Greta. This unnerved her a little.

She put her hand to the swinging door, paused, and turned around. "You wouldn't happen to have a scraper, would you?"

"Whatever would you need that for?" Greta's eyes zeroed in on Nina. Combined with her long nose, the look was positively hawk-like.

"I thought it would be nice to scrape off the newspaper plastered to the attic windows," Nina said. "Let in sunlight while I clean, offer a nice view." What at first was a simple request, she started to second-guess. Why had Greta covered up the windows to begin with?

Greta worked her jaw, still eyeing Nina intently, then nodded. She rose, tugged open a rattling drawer, withdrew a scraper, and placed it in Nina's outstretched hand. "Be gentle on the panes, will you?" A kind of nostalgic gleam softened Greta's intensity. Something about that room brought up emotions from Greta that she was clearly trying to suppress. "They're part of the original structure. I'd hate for them to get scratched."

"Of *course*," Nina replied. She jogged over to give Holden one last kiss, then exited the kitchen.

Upon entering the foyer, she took in a breath. Part of her was looking forward to the work. It gave her something to focus on. She made a mental note to check in with Greta and Holden within an hour or two. Surely, Holden would want food and a nap by then. The time between breastfeedings always gave her a burst of motivation as if she were racing against the clock—which she guessed she was.

Nina ascended the stairs, the stale air in the house growing warmer. It was the time of year in New York when one had to survive a couple of hot weeks without air conditioning. Wiping away a few strands of sweaty hair that had gotten in her eyes, she hoped the attic windows might open at least a crack. Otherwise, she was doomed to swelter. Perhaps she'd be able to find a floor fan, or something like it, among all the dusty items up here.

At last, she reached the top landing and stood in front of the door. She flinched at the memory of racing to slam it shut and leaning against it. It certainly didn't feel like it'd happened yesterday. The air swam around her like slow, heavy molasses. She sniffed and smelled a world filled with someone else's memories—mothballs, a hint of mildew, and, underlying it all, the sweet smell of what she was fairly certain was pollen.

She juggled to carry all the rags, gloves, scraper, and scarf under her right arm. It would take another trip to the nearby bathroom for water, buckets, and cleaning agents. With a grimace, Nina nudged the door open, ready to shut it at the first sign of more bees.

The sturdy door creaked open, revealing the space almost exactly as she'd left it yesterday. She moved over to what she suspected was a table, keeping an eye out for any flying, darting movement. Carefully, she removed the sheet covering the flat surface and laid it to the ground. She would use it to collect other dirty objects that needed cleaning or tossing, making it easier to cart them down to the laundry, wherever that was.

Beneath the sheet was a gleaming, handmade end table made of oak—a nice, tall platform with enough space to set out her gear. She wished she'd brought a glass of water. No matter. If she got desperate enough, she could drink some water from the sink, or wait and get some in the kitchen when she took a break in a couple of hours.

She slipped on the gloves, tied the scarf around her hairline, and armed herself with the scraper. With eight five-by-five, four-paned windows, she imagined it would take her most of the morning to scrape off the old, plastered newspaper.

She got to work.

9

Nina worked her way through the menial task with heartening ease. A few minutes into scraping, the initial unsettling feelings about the attic faded into the background. Layers of ancient newspaper lay in curls at the window bases, and on the floor. As she uncovered each windowpane, she discovered they were indeed a rich honey hue.

Instead of diminishing the view of the orchard fields, it enhanced them. Rows and rows of gilded apple trees bowed with grace under the weight of the ripening fruit they bore. The hill flowed downward, an elegant extension of the farmhouse into tall golden grasses, wildly untamed and hugging the tree trunks. A rosy sun had woken strong from its slumber, and colors mingled into a magnificent sangria shade in the skies above Orchard Hill.

After what Nina supposed was about an hour and a half, she looked up and saw she'd cleared seven of eight windows. She went to the doorway and listened for any indication that Holden might need her. When she heard soft giggles and Greta's voice, she relaxed her shoulders. She removed one glove to scratch her nose, then replaced it and approached the last window.

As she started in on one corner, she noticed the lettering on these newspapers was a touch darker. Though she'd tried to read the others, years of sun beating against the paper had caused the ink to fade into illegibleness. But on this window, the roof corner had provided more shade and protection.

Curiosity getting the better of her, Nina cupped her hands to the window and tried to discern what was written. Perhaps she might learn a stray tidbit about the town, an annual festival, local gossip, even a year and date that would give her a clue as to when this papier-mâché covering was put up. Did Greta do this?

The date of the paper eluded her. In fact, though the letters were darker, it divulged little in the way of information. Only one scrap in an article looked like it might be readable, yet the lettering was shadowed in duplicate. Nina puzzled over the article before stepping back and biting her lip.

Nodding, she decided what to do. It might not work, but she'd try anyway—she removed the gloves and set them and the scraper back onto the end table. Then, positioning herself in front of the window, she used the tip of her fingernail to tease back only the topmost layer of newspaper. She worked away the corner and almost removed the entire layer over the article when there was a *bang* behind her.

The attic door had slammed shut.

Nina started. She gulped, then made a sound between a relieved sigh and a laugh. The heat in the attic had grown unbearable halfway through clearing off the windows, and she'd indeed been able to open a window. The panes were the type that could rotate vertically on hinges, so they wouldn't open all the way, just an inch or two. It'd been enough to alleviate some of the heat and apparently had also been enough to cause a draft that blew the door closed.

Holding a hand to her chest to still her excited heart, Nina stooped forward to get a better look at the words she'd uncovered. The headline read: "The Mysterious Widow of Orchard Hill." There was a picture underneath, supposedly Orchard Hill farm-house, but it was so distorted in black-and-gray splotches that it looked like an amorphous shadow of itself.

The beginning of the article read:

Greta Richardson, 41 years old, of Orchard Hill, is now the official owner of the house and property, after being made a widow upon Henry Richardson's death at age 45. Despite speculation around town to the contrary, the official statement from the police was that Mr. Richardson died as a result of an allergic reaction to a bee sting. However, his medical records did not indicate a history of this allergy.

Orchard Hill is famous for having one of the largest bee colonies in the area, and Mrs. Richardson herself is sometimes referred to as the "Queen of Bees." One townsperson, who asked to remain anonymous, specu-lated that Mrs. Richardson might have reason to want her husband dead—

It was there the article was cut off. Nina's mouth went dry. Not knowing what to make of it, she vigor-ously scraped away the final scraps of paper from the last window. In a huff, she let the scraper fall from her hand to clang on the floor amongst the spent shavings. She rubbed her upper arms, an unnaturally cool breeze tickling her skin. Rumors are rumors, she told herself. It's not like she hadn't felt the same way about John. Maybe not want him dead exactly. But gone? Definitely.

She stared out over the unmarred landscape, the apple trees robust with green leaves sparkling in the sun. The view was as breathtaking as she'd imagined, and she felt the satisfaction of a job well done. It was a shame Greta didn't open the orchard to the public for apple picking, or hire a crew to harvest them. Such a great activity for this warming and blooming time of year.

One of Nina's few happy family moments was when she, John, and Holden—still growing inside her belly—went apple picking. The scent of fallen, overripe apples, eager to start the season, reached her nose and beckoned. Nina licked her lips. It occurred to her that sinking her teeth into a fresh apple was something she'd desired the moment she saw Orchard Hill. Maybe Greta would let her pick a basketful, and they could make a pie later.

The isolation of this land was all-encompassing, simultaneously terrifying and thrilling her with its freedom.

Nina turned reluctantly to the door. Her arms ached for Holden, and she wanted to plant kisses all over his big cheeks. Funny, the dichotomies of motherhood, how she was always desperate for a moment's peace, yet missing her child just as desperately when he wasn't there.

She halted at movement outside the window.

Out of sync with the wind in the trees, a dark, disjointed shape had caught her eye. She rushed to the window, braced her hands on the sill, pressed her nose against the glass. It couldn't be *him*.

Could it?

Every fiber of her being said it was John, come to drag her and Holden home. Nina blinked, questioned her eyesight, her sanity. She pressed her palm to her forehead, feeling unsteady on her feet. It'd been some time since she'd had anything to drink, losing herself in the cleaning and forgetting to make a trip to the bathroom downstairs to refresh her mouth with water. She might just be dizzy, fatigued.

Yet as soon as she felt ready to move, and was reasonably sure she wouldn't faint, Nina rushed to close the window she'd opened, then darted down the stairs. If there was any chance that John was sneaking up on the house, she wanted to make damn sure he wouldn't touch a hair on Holden's head.

"Whatever is the matter, child?" Greta asked, cradling Holden on her lap on the daisy-speckled couch in the front parlor. "You look like you've had a good fright."

After spending over a day in Greta's company, Nina was getting used to the woman's eyebrows and their permanent, upward stitch of questioning amusement.

"I thought—" Nina opened and closed her mouth a couple of times, catching her breath and trying to determine how much she should share. It was an unspoken understanding between the two women that Nina had left her husband. Possibly, Greta even suspected some sort of abuse, especially considering the bruising on Nina's face.

But it didn't seem wise, telling the woman that her abusive husband (by the way, also a cop!) was likely hunting her down. The look of pity in Greta's eyes brought into focus how crazy it was to think that John would actually find her all the way out here, in the middle of nowhere.

Nina plopped down on the couch next to them and stroked Holden's hair. Though she kept her eyes warily glued to the front yard, she sighed.

"Nevermind," she said. "It was nothing."

10

Nina evaded what weren't exactly questions but sly comments from Greta in an effort to get more out of Nina, to get at what had frightened her. From the insinuations, Nina thought Greta chalked it up to a stray bee and an overreaction. As for Nina herself, after a long evening rife with nightmares that left her tossing and turning, she couldn't deny that, in John's absence, her imagination had gone haywire, and she'd fallen victim to no more than shadow-play.

The next morning, instead of heading up to the attic to continue cleaning, Nina asked Greta if she could explore the orchard with Holden, and maybe pick apples to make a pie together later. Greta seemed eager to do some work of her own, and they parted ways.

Nina scrounged up a wicker basket with a handle and fleece blanket from the front hall closet. In addition to several women's coats in Greta's style, there were other coats in there too—quite a few men's coats that looked like they hadn't been used in decades. Nina shrugged. They probably hadn't been, if they belonged to Greta's husband, Henry.

Was that part of the reason the attic was emotional for Greta? Nina couldn't imagine what it would be like to go through and discard the material things left behind, the pitiful summation of a life, by someone who was close to you, whether or not you were still fond of them. Memories could be like quicksand, and she understood why Greta might want to avoid falling into those pits.

Despite a fitful sleep, Nina felt decently replenished. This bolstered her confidence, and she was determined to prove to herself that no one was stalking her from the orchard. Though the only way she slept at all was because she'd had no energy left after the work, caring for Holden later in the day, and her frazzled nerves. That, and the chair she'd wedged underneath the door, ensuring no intruders could get in without causing a ruckus, sure to wake her up. She did, however, vaguely recall waking again in the night to the sound of something in the walls, and figured she'd add laying out mousetraps to her itinerary.

Before heading out the front door, Nina paused at the sight of a wooden, hand-carved cane by the door. In a last-minute decision, she tucked the cane under her arm. It could come in handy if she were wrong, and she needed to defend herself. The idea of taking John on one-on-one drained the blood from her face.

Once outside, she left that thought behind as the bright, warm sunshine caressed her cheeks. Holden giggled at a dragonfly that zipped by. It put a smile on her face, and together, they set off down the hill. Soon, they disappeared into the huddled crowds of apple trees, branches curtsying to expose their shiny red apples. Nina spread out the blanket on a clear patch of grass and set Holden upon it to explore while she gathered the basket in the crook of her arm and turned to the nearest tree.

"Holden, aren't these pretty? We're in what's called an orchard, and this is an apple tree." Over her shoulder, she continued to cast frequent glances to make sure Holden wasn't getting into anything that might hurt him. Sometimes she felt ridiculous, talking so much to someone who couldn't talk back. But she'd read in a book that it was really good for speech development, so she kept it up despite being tired of her own voice. "I'm picking apples to make us a pie later. Mmm."

Raising onto her tippy toes, Nina reached for a particularly fat apple. She grasped it, twisted it at the stem, and plucked it off into her hand. Holden watched her intently and worked to get to his feet to come closer. Stooping down, Nina rubbed the apple on her shirt and presented it to him as he toddled to her.

The little boy grabbed for the apple and opened his mouth as wide as he could. With only two bottom teeth, Nina wouldn't bet on much of a bite. She let loose her grip on the apple so he could play with it. When he seemed satisfied, turning it over curiously in his tiny hands, Nina resumed picking at the others.

Lazy clouds coasted by, softening the heat. Nina was thankful to the light breeze for keeping the temperature bearable.

In no time, her basket was overflowing, and she turned back to Holden. "Okay, monkey, I think that's about enough sun for you—"

Nina dropped the basket, the apples scattering everywhere at her feet.

Except for the apple, the blanket was empty.

She tried to reason with herself. She'd only looked away for a second. Was that even true? And who was she trying to justify her actions to, anyway? She knew that it only took a second for a toddler to get into some serious trouble.

"Holden!" she yelled. Nina made a mad dash around the immediate trees, hoping to spot a glimpse of his playground-yellow onesie. Was that the one with the duck on it? Sweat trickled down her back. She stomped through grassy undergrowth and shoved away tree branches that slapped her in the face, wishing she'd chosen a better outfit. When she didn't find Holden right away, she darted back to the blanket and brandished the cane in front of her.

The clouds parted, leaving only the piercing blue above the trees. The sounds of nature around her magnified and congealed into a heavy blanket of buzzing until she yearned to clamp her hands over her ears.

"I know you're there!" Sweat stung her eyes, clouded her vision. Her skin flushed at the heat, and she longed to peel off her sticky clothes.

Branches jostled nearby that definitely weren't caused by wind or natural occurrence.

"John," she said. "If you promise not to hurt Holden, I'll come back."

The words were bitter acid on her tongue. The cane quivered in her shaking hands. In the tall, unkempt grass, Nina glimpsed a flash of yellow. In her desperation, Nina discarded the cane onto the blanket and sprinted through the trees.

The buzzing droned in her ears. She bit the inside of her lip, probably drawing blood, but all she could think about was getting to her son. Having lost sight of Holden's onesie, she stopped and pivoted madly, whirling around for any sight of him. All she saw was the same, the same and more of the same—apple trees in an overgrown, untended orchard, such that she wasn't even certain if she really was turning around. Having never intended to go this deep into the orchard, she had no clue how far she'd gone.

"Holden! Holden!" Nina called through cupped hands. "Please! Come to Momma!"

All movement stopped. With the blank blue sky and no wind to ruffle leaves in the trees, Nina had the impression of being frozen in some macabre painting, overly idyllic and indifferent to her distress. The buzzing rose to a sharp crescendo that snapped in her ears, then ceased all at once. One by one, the routine nature sounds resumed, first with the chirping of the crickets, then the trill of the birds, the wind once more brushing across the leaves.

Just when Nina thought her heart might shrivel and give up on her, it swelled to bursting at the sounds of Holden's babbling. Like a house cat trying to put her underdeveloped outdoor skills to use, Nina carefully picked over an especially dense clump of rotten apples, their stench sickeningly sweet, to make her way closer to the sounds of her son.

Trunks bent inward like crones, the branches contorted, knitted tightly. Save for a few hazy sunbeams offering only weak light and menacing silhouettes, light failed to penetrate this part of the orchard.

Nina crouched to maneuver closer to the call of her child. She found herself at the edge of a clearing that formed the intersection of four great apple trees, all gnarled and veiled by jade green leaves. Their roots snaked through the underbrush, coiled and knotted in places. This place exuded an aura more ancient than the farmhouse. Were these the original trees of Orchard Hill?

At the nexus of the haggard trees teetered Holden, grass as high as his chubby thighs. Happy as a clam, he flailed his arms excitedly, babbling in the direction of one of the gnarled trunks. As Nina drew closer, forced to slow so as not to twist an ankle on the wild roots, pain flared from the bee sting on her arm. Steadily stepping faster now, she clamped one hand over the wound. Her stomach filled with the leaden dread of realizing Holden's attention was directed approximately six feet above him . . . about John's height.

Nina followed Holden's gaze and stared into those stirring shadows until a face formed. She gasped, held still. Panic played havoc with her heart. Seconds ticked away until she blinked, uncertain what she saw. It could have been the features of a man. It could also have been the wrinkled bark of a decades-old apple tree.

"Holden, sweetie." She held out her hand to him. Usually this got his attention. The 'figure,' whatever it was, in the trees was too interesting. Nina licked her dry, cracking lips and tried again. "Monkey," she called, knowing it was impossible to keep the tremor out of her voice.

Holden faced her with a bright smile. He ran into her arms, offering a wide open-mouthed kiss on her cheek. She scooped him up with a glare toward the cavernous darkness, and whatever lay among those decrepit trees.

"John," she said, surprised at the fortitude in her voice, "stop playing games. If you're in there, come on out, and we'll get this sorted."

Nina squeezed Holden flush against her torso as she inched as close as she dared to the curtain of dark emerald leaves. When she was a child, her mother wasn't afraid of anything. Now, she knew intimately that fear and worry coursed through a mother's veins, as plentiful as lifeblood. But a mother—any good mother—overcame by way of a love purer and stronger than any fear.

Her fingers trembled as Nina lifted a branch aside to get a glimpse at the inner recesses. Judging by the girth of the weathered trunk, she suspected this must've been the oldest of the four trees. The branch resisted her. Nina might've relented and headed back for the safety of the house but for two spots of lighter coloring, the ones she'd mistaken for glowering eyes, that shone against the near-black of the grizzled apple tree bark.

She dodged a root the size of a python and brushed her fingers over the spots. They were carvings in the bark, she realized, crudely drawn in the tree with a knife. One was a . . . G? Accompanied by a tiny plus sign and perhaps an O or a C.

When she exited the gloomy sanctum with Holden in her arms, the sunlight, glittering white diamonds across the landscape, nearly blinded her. Nina shielded against the onslaught with her free hand. Yet it took time for her eyes to adjust and even longer to reorient herself so that she could find their blanket, basket, and the cane.

Nina sighed and said a silent, if not reproachful, prayer to the house for guiding her way back home.

Home—such a funny word. What made a place a home, anyway?

Holden wiggled in her arms, growing fussy for food and rest. She trudged toward the house, rolling that word over in her mind. Nothing in her held much nostalgia for the ranch house she'd shared with John, except for the sweet-in-hindsight memories of Holden's newborn days. It certainly wasn't home anymore, if it had ever been.

Up ahead, with its looming body and slanted rooftops, Orchard Hill reflected too much of its owner's personality to feel homey. Nina hugged Holden to her breast and inhaled the intoxicating baby smell from his downy hair. Home wasn't about the place, she decided, it was about the people—the people you loved and who loved you.

As she walked, the sun warming her skin, making the darkened apple trees fade like a mirage in her thoughts, Nina conceded that perhaps a place could take on that unique quality of home if it were infused with the memories of those you loved, leaving an indelible imprint in the house, on the land.

She rubbed her forefingers together, recalling the roughly carved initials in the wood, and surmised that the G must belong to Greta. Yet who did the other initial belong to? Who would Greta love enough to impress that love permanently upon one of Orchard Hill's oldest trees? Because it certainly wasn't her husband, Henry.

11

Nina spent the rest of the day secluded in the farmhouse kitchen with Holden. What kind of cat-and-mouse game was John playing with her? No longer could she explain away these incidents as paranoia. Even if she were wrong, and on some level, she hoped she was. Letting her guard down had consequences she wasn't willing to suffer.

Between entertaining Holden and doing some deep cleaning in the kitchen, the afternoon sped by. The broad bay window above the kitchen sink looked out over the back of the property. About a hundred feet from the house, six rows of off-white boxes, tall as her hip, nestled in the grasses like large, square hen eggs. Greta was working among the boxes as graceful as a fencer in her stark white beekeeping gear. A bee buffeted the window, and Nina flinched. She set the plate down that had ages ago been dried by her hand towel, despite her continued motions.

The bird clock chirped above her head, and a cardinal announced the late hour. Nina figured she'd make herself useful and have dinner ready when Greta came back inside. It amazed her that such an elderly woman could work for so long, and in such hot weather. The honeycomb frames Greta lifted out back must've weighed a ton. Nina shook her head. She had no interest in getting up close and personal with the beehives herself to find out.

Now familiar with the contents of Greta's fridge and pantry, Nina rustled up the ingredients for piecrust. After putting the dough in the refrigerator to chill, she cooked up and shredded some chicken. In Greta's hardy old skillet, Nina sauteed chopped onions in butter and had fun with Holden, letting him 'help' her add peas, carrots, and potatoes to the mixture, along with chicken broth and milk. After it was done cooking, she added her chicken and spooned it into the piecrust. Nina hoped Greta would appreciate chicken pot pie for dinner. Nina's own mouth watered at the home-cooked smell, and her stomach rumbled in anticipation. Holden would never let her forget to feed him, and yet, somehow, feeding herself a bit of lunch had eluded her.

While Holden played by her feet with a pot and ladle, Nina perched on one of the island chairs. The past couple days had gone nothing like she'd envisioned. They should've been long on their way to her old high school friend's house, having a quick awkward conversation with Bobbi, perhaps getting a night job at a fast-food place and begging her friend to help care for Holden in the evenings along with their own children.

How had she let herself get so far off track? She and Holden didn't belong here. They needed to get far away from Orchard Hill, from John, and stop bringing trouble to an old woman's doorstep.

Nina rose abruptly, her chair wobbling. Greta might be able to give her enough pay for the couple of day's work and a ride into town that would help get them moving on. She'd find her way to Bobbi's, one way or another. Anything but staying here.

Holden tugged on her dress. She glanced down at him and made up her mind. Though it churned her stomach to think about how hard it might be, she had to believe they'd make it, so she could provide a good life for Holden, free from danger and worry. When Greta came in tonight, she'd thank her for her kind offer but request a ride back to town.

Nina struggled to swallow past the ill-tasting film that'd formed in her mouth. She hustled over to the sink, swiped a glass from the cabinet, and held it under the tap. She chugged the water in large gulps when she heard the now-familiar squeal of the revolving kitchen door behind her.

"Smells good." Greta came over and leaned the small of her back against the counter, looking sidelong at her. Nina marveled at how nothing in Greta's face or stance showed the exhausting day's work she'd just put in.

"It's the least I could do to repay you for these last couple of days," Nina said. "I really appreciate your offer, but—"

"It doesn't smell like apples." Greta sniffed the air and tapped the side of her nose.

"What?" Nina asked.

"Well, wasn't that what you were doing this morning?" Greta waved her hands low and matter-of-factly. "You and that sweet boy went out into the orchard to pick some apples, bake a pie."

Holden whined. Nina offered him a sip of water from the edge of her cup, careful to hold the glass, so he didn't tip or drop it. It was adorable how he tried to drink out of it like a big boy, and she was always amused when he swallowed several gulps with an over-eagerness that caused him to sputter and cough. "Oh, right. About that—"

Greta pushed off the counter and stood over Nina, imposing and judging. "Now, child, I've done my best to respect your privacy and not pry. But I think it's time you were upfront with me. Clearly, you're frightened. Do I need to rustle up the old rifle and have it ready?"

Nina's eyes widened. "A gun?" Nina settled Holden into the high chair, then went to pull the chicken pot pie out of the oven before the crust burned. "No, no guns. I'm not comfortable with guns around my son."

With good reason, after Holden had accidentally picked up John's sidearm one day. Luckily, she'd gotten it from him before anything had happened. She kept this to herself, still finding reasons it was unwise to share with Greta that John was a cop. Though those reasons were becoming less and less compelling.

Greta pressed closer into Nina's personal space. Her breath ran sweet, off-putting like she'd been eating honey all day. Nina wrinkled her nose.

"I understand that," Greta said. Her eyes fell on Nina's healing bruises. "But to protect her child, a mother sometimes has to do things that make her uncomfortable."

Nina brushed past Greta and began feeding Holden his dinner. Who was this woman to tell her what she ought and ought not to do for her son?

Nina blew on a heaping spoonful of the steaming food to cool it. When Greta's bony fingers touched her shoulder, she spun around before Greta could say anything.

"I'm not even going to entertain what you're sug-
gesting, Greta," Nina said. "It's unthinkable. I don't
care what you've done. I don't care about your opin-
ions on how I should mother my child. That man
has done enough harm. The last thing I'm going to
do is let him make me a monster."

Nina returned to feeding Holden, who'd gone
wide-eyed and silent at her stern tone. She stroked
his hair and kissed his head to assure him everything was okay.

From behind her, Greta's voice, normally terse
and prim, was unsteady and distant. "And what is it
you think I've done?"

Holden was a fast eater, which usually frustrated
Nina, as it gave her no time to do anything else
while he ate. Tonight, though, she was thankful.
Nina sighed and went over to wet a paper towel at
the sink to wipe Holden down. Not facing the
woman, Nina spoke evenly. "I saw the article."

With that, Nina scooped Holden up in her arms
and strode across the kitchen to the door. She
turned back to Greta. "We'd appreciate a ride back
to town in the morning."

"Wait, Nina—"

Nina didn't wait to hear what Greta had to say.
She had more than she could handle in one day and
just wanted to get to bed and cuddle with her son.

When Nina nudged open the door to the guest
room, she was met with the crib from the attic set up
at her bedside, complete with a soft green blanket
and Holden's stuffed stegosaurus. Her shoulders
drooped under the weight of exhaustion and sorrow.
She changed Holden, brushed their teeth, and sang
him a soothing lullaby while she mulled over the
day's events.

She longed for a simpler world, a place where people were less complicated, all good or all bad. Like the westerns she used to watch while snuggling up with her dad on the couch, where the good cowboys wore stars and the outlaws had black hats. Her life couldn't be further from that fantasy.

When John was awful, it hurt more than she could bear. And yet, all that surfaced now were the reasons she stayed with him. The unexpected ways he could be sweet, if he wanted to, surprising her with daffodils, kisses, and tenderness, given so sparsely that she was like a starving woman, dependent, easily lured right back in.

What a fright he'd given her today. It had to have been him in the orchard field, right? Otherwise, who was Holden talking to? Looking down into Holden's sleepy face, she debated what was best for him, and just didn't know. Should a boy have his father, no matter what? Was she right to take that away from him? Again she longed for straightforward answers, and felt betrayed when neither heart nor mind provided them.

As she set Holden down in the crib that Greta had so nicely brought down for them, she reflected on the woman's actions. This was another person who could be sweet one moment and cold the next. It was true Nina made giant leaps about the nature of Greta's past. Perhaps she should give the woman a chance to explain. The newspaper did say her husband had died of a bee sting. How could Greta have been responsible for that? Although the older woman carried around a mummified queen bee in a vial around her neck, which was, at best, highly strange and, at worst, highly suspicious, Nina vowed

to have an open mind, if only to honor the lesson of
Ms. Keeler.

Nina's stomach growled, admonishing her for
skipping yet another meal. With Holden safely in a
crib and already on his way to sleepy town, his arms
wrapped around Stego, she figured she could risk a
trip down to the kitchen to heat up some of the leftover pot pie. She was reasonably sure she would
hear him if he woke up and started crying. She'd
only be one floor down.

She crept downstairs, unsure whether she
wanted to find Greta still awake and perhaps willing
to talk, or if she'd rather just eat her pot pie in silence. All the lights, save one by the back door, were
off. Relief washed over at not having to dive into a
deep conversation after all the emotional distress of
the day. The twinge of disappointment might be satisfied tomorrow morning. Besides, it was probably a
conversation best left until after some food and rest.

Nina flicked on the oven in the old kitchen—
Greta lacked a microwave—and scooped out some
pot pie into a baking pan. While she waited for the
food to warm up, she went to the sink to get a cup of
water. As she brought the cup to her lips, she froze
halfway through a sip.

Out back, behind Orchard Hill farmhouse, a
blood-red light floated among the rows of beehives,
weaving through in a silent procession. Nina made
out Greta's slender, stiff-backed figure holding a fat
red candle in her hands, the solitary flame casting
sharp angles on Greta's face. Tension coiled in
Nina's body. A distant ache echoed in her jaw from
involuntarily clenching her teeth, aggravating her
bruise, not fully healed.

Nina fumbled with her glass to place it on the

counter, spilling some, and snuck over to the back door for a better view. She thought the light from the candle would've reflected off the cream white of the painted boards on the bee boxes. Yet all Nina saw was black like Greta had covered them with something. Nina glanced over her shoulder and listened for Holden. Hearing nothing, she carefully twisted the door handle and opened the door a sliver.

A mournful melody drifted over the swaying, knee-high grass to Nina's ears. Greta sang with a sadness that reverberated deep into the marrow of every bone in Nina's body:

Oh, what small mercy can this be?

Have you found it in your heart to forgive me?

Gone, you are not, and so the bees I have not told

Though my house, my body, my soul have grown old

Ripe with life and love, apples are birthed from the trees

Mother and son have come; I'll be brought to my knees

For what's true is strange and thy honey, sweet

And I fear we'll part before we can ever again meet

Nina caught a whiff of burning pie, smokey and acrid. She gasped. Greta's head jerked at the sound, and for several breathless moments, Nina was sure she was caught. Then Greta continued her bizarre and curious ritual, and Nina gently shut the door and rushed over to the oven. By the time she was done dealing with the burned pie, Greta and her red candle were no longer visible outside.

Nina brushed strands of hair out of her face, the somber song lingering in her mind. She sighed as she trudged over to the fridge. There wasn't any use

trying to make sense of the lyrics—sad words from a
sad old woman. And yet, it was interesting that
Greta had alluded to herself and Holden.

Still ravenous, Nina grabbed from the crisper
one of the apples she'd picked from the orchard earlier that day. As she climbed the stairs, she bit into
the shiny red flesh as ripe with life and love as Greta
described. Nothing she'd ever eaten had tasted so
sweet.

12

Tossing and turning later that night, Nina rolled over with an exasperated sigh. She hated when phantom baby cries ruined her sleep, a phenomenon that seemed to increase with stress. Holden snoozed safely, not two feet from her in the crib. She resisted the urge to touch him, confirm his presence.

Now that she was awake, her bladder refused to let her fall back asleep. Nina threw aside the covers and crossed the hallway into the bathroom. After she was done, she stood in the hall for a moment. Moonlight filtered in through the gauzy, tan curtains at the end of the hall, casting pools of milky-brown light like molasses on the oak flooring.

Nina took two steps forward to the guest room and stopped. She laid her hand on the closed door and searched her memory for whether she'd actually closed it. It seemed unlikely that she would've closed it with Holden still inside. She gripped the doorknob—it didn't budge. Alarm bells rang in her head.

She rubbed away the sleep in her eyes, certain it

must just be the fog of the middle of the night con-
fusing her. Nina peered down the hall toward the
staircase and blinked rapidly. A mental count of the
doors told her there were far too many. The longer
she looked, the further the corridor stretched, like
coffee-colored taffy.

Nina jiggled the doorknob again, to no avail.
The nightly buzzing sound started to the left of the
door and traveled away from her, like the mur-
muring of a million faraway voices. Nina pressed
her ear to the wall and walked sidelong, following
the sound, with only the vague idea that she might
find its source. And if she could find it, maybe she
could find a way back inside the room to her son.

The buzzing traveled faster and faster, until she
was jogging at a pretty good clip to keep up. She
couldn't fathom the length the hallway would need
to be for her to run down it this far and fast. Soon,
Nina was calling out to Greta, to Holden—even, ab-
surdly, to John.

No one answered her.

Nina's hands and feet grew numb and, despite
just relieving herself, she felt pressure in her
bladder again. She wanted to stop, to slow down, to
think. And yet the buzzing would not relent. Her
breath came out in ragged heaves, a stitch forming
in her side.

Nina did the only thing she could think to do.
She started slapping and banging on the wood paneling, hoping to provoke and confront whatever was
taunting her from inside the farmhouse walls. As
she did so, a realization emerged—she no longer
ran down the hallway in a straight line.

Each time she finished one full length of the

hallway, it pivoted and repeated itself. It was hard to tell, but it might've been in an octagon shape, not unlike the shape of the attic room. She dared to stop, and proceeded to kick and punch the wall to the left of the guest room door with blind fury until it dented and broke. A cloying smell poured forth from the small, dank opening. She recoiled, coughing, before resuming her attack.

Slivers of wood lashed her hands. Her cries of frustration curdled into screams of pain, her hands slick with her own blood. The walls oozed a thick, viscous substance that coated her forearms and chest as she tore away segment after segment of wood, revealing saccharine darkness in the walls.

At last, Nina opened a hole large enough for her arm. Without thinking, she shoved her hand inside, the wood scraping her wrist. She sought the interior doorknob, anything to let her in, to make sure Holden was alright. Instead, her fingers plunged into a squirming mass, alive and crawling. Repulsed, she snatched her hand from the hole and, with morbid fascination, brought it up to her face, inspecting it in the sugar-brown moonlight.

Her hand was smeared with thick, sweet liquid. *Honey.*

A sensation like thousands of prickly needles erupted from her palm. The droning rose to a thunderous crescendo. Turning up her palm, her mouth hung wide in horror at the furry black-and-yellow bodies covering her hand like a glove.

Each bee exposed its stinger and, in unison, plunged them deep into her flesh.

That's when Nina screamed—and awoke.

Late morning sunlight streamed through the

guest bedroom window. She hadn't awoken in the night. It was just a dream.

She breathed. However, a new fear quickly supplanted the lingering horror and phantom pain of the bee stings. Something was wrong in her room. Unwillingly, she craned her neck to confirm what she already knew to be true.

Holden was not in his crib.

Nina burst out of her room and raced down the hall, still clad in her linen pajamas. She reeled from the experience of the blurred hallway—so like her dream—and snapped herself back to reality as fast as she could muster.

"Greta, you can't keep doing this!"

Her heart pounded in her chest. She took the stairs down to the foyer two at a time and nearly rolled her ankle on the last step. She had expected the sounds of Holden from the kitchen and the smells of breakfast cooking in the air. Her hands shook uncontrollably as she met with nothing. This time felt different, too, jarring and wrong, the emotional equivalent of a dislocated limb.

Nina entered the kitchen, heralded by the screech of the rusty hinges on the swinging door. The large iron appliances sat slumbering and cold. Even the oven's face looked like a big frown to her. Before she continued her frantic search of the house and the yards, something on the counter caught her eye.

Like a cruel joke, a black-and-yellow-striped thermos weighed down the edge of a note. Nina plucked it from the counter and read:

Dearest Nina,

Holden and I are out picking apples. Please don't worry, I wanted to give you some space to think.

*We're more alike than you know. I just don't want
you to make the same mistakes I did.*

*I hope you can relax with this tea I've made for you.
I'll be back in a jiffy. Then you and I can have a little
chat about what you're going to do.*

Sincerely,

Greta

"The gall of that woman!" Her mind whirred like
an overworked motor. Without thinking, she seized
the thermos and downed the tea in angry gulps. The
sweet, fiery liquid singed her tongue, and she spat it
out onto the tile floor. Nina rolled her tongue
around in her mouth and spit some more, doing
anything to get the sweet taste out of her mouth.

"*Honey,*" Nina seethed.

It was the last straw. She'd have felt better if
Greta had been actually trying to poison her. Anything but this.

Every second gone by was another that Holden
was alone with this madwoman. The notion was like
a weight of bricks crashing down upon her.

She pivoted too fast, and her ankle protested.
Where did Greta keep the phone? Nina racked her
brain—in the foyer. On the entryway table. Yes. If
she didn't find Holden or something happened to
her, she needed to know someone would save him
from Greta.

She dialed her mother's number from memory,
swallowing a lump in her throat.

It rang once, twice, three times, each ring a kick
to the gut.

"Hello?" John's baritone voice wafted through
the receiver. His breath was like that of a dog that
you weren't sure was going to lick you, snarl, or
lash out.

Nina opened her mouth to speak. Not a sound emerged. She'd known it'd been a risk to try her mother, but had hoped he hadn't gone to her yet. Bile rose in the back of her throat.

"Honey? Is that you?" The softness in his voice almost coaxed the words out of her mouth.

Silence.

"You can't take my son from me like this, Nina. Come home this minute or I'll—"

Nina slammed the phone down and it rattled off the hook and landed on the floor. Her hands shook as she picked it up and put it back in the cradle. Hearing his voice, she thought of an oblong case she'd seen in the attic, about ten inches thick. Just like the ones John kept his rifles in.

She bounded up the stairs. When she arrived at the attic doorway, she leaned her forearm against the doorjamb, rubbing her fingers at the stitch in her side. She tried not to think about how it was the same stitch she'd felt in her dream.

She tore through the attic room, shoving aside old chairs and tables, dolls and clothes on her way to her intended target. Sweaty strands of hair fell in her face as she kneeled before the case. Nina flinched as it clicked open, easily responding to her fingers' light touch, despite the heavy coating of dust on its lid. Inside gleamed a long rifle with a wooden stock.

Lifting the gun up, she cringed at the solid weight of it in her hands. No one could live with her husband and not develop a familiarity with guns. She checked the chamber—empty—then pressed the butt of the gun into her shoulder, and hurried downstairs and out the front door.

She would never actually shoot Greta or anyone, for that matter, but Greta didn't need to know that. Either way, she was going to get her son and get the hell out of there.

13

When she entered the orchard, it was like she'd never left from the day before. Again, not a cloud in sight. Her feet carried her with a mind of their own all the way back to the oldest trees in the orchard. She cried out to Holden.

On the outskirts of the eerie sanctuary of craggy trees, Nina's adrenaline faded fast. No one answered her calls, and her son was nowhere in sight. Her eyes welled with tears, and her arms burned with the weight of the gun.

She lowered it as a single cloud encased her in shadow. Tears streamed down Nina's cheeks. Greta. John. She couldn't give up. She had to be strong for Holden, but she wasn't sure she could carry on.

Behind her, the snap of a branch. She started, raised the gun, and swiveled around. "Who's there? Show yourself."

Another heavy crack. Movement of a dark figure cast away all doubt that someone was there. She bit her lip to stop it from quivering. Jamming the stock of the gun deeper into her shoulder, she tracked the movements as something big stalked from within the ancient trees. Nina was dimly aware that the normal sounds of nature once again receded into the background. Loud static took over. Her eyes burned, demanding she blink, yet she didn't dare for fear of losing sight of the dark silhouette among the evergreen leaves.

"John, is that you?" She'd called her mother's cell, so he could be anywhere.

At the sound of her voice, the tall figure circled her faster and faster until she couldn't keep up without spinning herself into dizziness.

"John, I swear to God if you touch a hair on our boy's head, I'll—" Shoot him? *Kill* him? No, she couldn't do that. She swung the gun barrel around and slammed into someone with all the give of a steel beam. The person snatched her weapon and swiftly knocked her down.

Dazed, Nina raised a defensive hand. The sun backlit the approaching figure. Her heart bashed against her ribcage. Her eyes were desperate to adjust to the light. The first thing she noticed was that this man had blonde hair, not black. She squinted and saw a hand outstretched, offering to help her up. Nina debated whether to swat it away or take it, then finally took the man's hand.

Strong and lean and definitely not her husband, the handsome stranger lifted her with ease and held her close against his chest before releasing her. She ignored a fluttering in her that had nothing to do with fear and everything to do with unmet needs.

"Who the hell are you?" Nina stammered.

Before her stood a well-built man, not far from her own age, late twenties perhaps, with steel-gray eyes as discerning as a cat, and a face that would make any woman blush at his gaze.

The man held his hands out, as if she were a

wild animal that would run away at any sudden movement. He propped Nina's rifle against one of the old tree trunks and returned to her. "I'm sorry, ma'am. Did I give you a fright?"

Nina laughed and pressed her hand to her heart. "What do you think?" Her eyes darted to the rifle.

"I heard you yelling and thought you were in some kind of trouble. My name is Colin."

Nina watched him run a nervous hand through his hair. The fluttering returned. "I'm sorry too, then. I could've sworn there was someone in these trees." She rubbed her hands on her linen pajamas, shrugging in embarrassment at the state of herself. "Nina. I'm staying with Greta, helping her around the house. She didn't mention anyone else on the orchard."

Colin offered his hand to her. It was warm and strong as she clasped it. "I'm a farmhand. Greta hires me sometimes to help keep up with things around the orchard. I don't imagine that she likes to admit to needing help every now and again."

Nina nodded. "I can see that."

They chuckled together at this. Then, Colin raised an eyebrow at her. "So, you say there was someone in these trees?"

Nina sighed. "Maybe I was just letting the orchard get the best of me." She became aware that she was staring at Colin's handsome face a bit too long and looked away, her mind never having fully left behind the fact that Holden was still somewhere with Greta.

"Is something else troubling you, Nina?" Colin's gentle hand on her shoulder almost broke her.

She turned to face him and nearly had to press her hands against his chest at how close he was.

Nina took two steps back and scratched the side of her head. "I'm looking for Greta. She took my son out into the orchard, and I, uh, just want to check on them."

It was odd that she was self-conscious about how Colin would react to the news of her having a son. She hadn't found herself in a situation where she cared what a man thought of her in a very long time.

"Sure. Anything to allay a mother's worries." He smirked at her and offered the crook of his arm. She slipped a tentative hand around his firm bicep, the touch electric on her skin. He escorted her through the orchard. "I think I saw them just over here."

"Thank you." When she smiled at him, he beamed back at her.

After a few minutes of pleasant silence between them, Colin nudged her. "You know, if you're worried about Greta, there's really no need to be."

Nina paused. She was surprised when she let him wipe a stray tear off her cheek, and run his thumb between her brows to ease the worry. "Is that so? I don't really know much about her."

Colin offered his arm again, and they resumed walking. "Greta doesn't always make all the right decisions and isn't necessarily my favorite person in the world."

"But?"

Colin worked his shoulders back and dipped his head to her. Though this strange man was so kind and gentle with her, she wasn't sure if she could trust it, endearing though it was. "But . . . Greta has a good heart. She would never do anything to hurt you or your son. She's a lonely, old woman with a wretched past. She had a . . . husband who wasn't good to her. I believe it left behind a stain."

Stain.

The image of her own blood-stained pillow, in the bedroom once shared with John, came back to her. Colin gave her room to think about this. He was different from so many others who eagerly wanted to fill the silence.

"Yes, I understand something about stains," she said at last.

He only nodded as they came to the edge of the trees. There, in the side yard, Greta sat on a blanket, playing with Holden. Her baby's giggles floated to Nina like wind chimes on the air, and it was all she could do to not run to him.

She turned back to Colin, shaking his hand as she gazed into his piercing-gray eyes. The nightmare, the anger at Greta's note, the call to John, all of that faded like mist in sunlight. She'd been a ball of anxiety, yet something about Colin calmed her greatly. Nina couldn't help herself—she wanted more of that feeling, a sureness in herself, that everything was going to be alright.

"Thank you, Colin," she said. "Maybe I'll see you again tomorrow?"

Colin gave her a heart-stopping, knee-knocking smile. With the tip of an imaginary hat, he retreated into the orchard and said, "Count on it, Nina."

With that, he was gone.

14

After putting Holden down for his morning nap, Nina came out onto the front porch, where Greta had a tray of tea ready. Nina sat next to her on one of the wingback wicker chairs that creaked as she sat down. Under the awning, and aided by a soft breeze, the maturing day had turned out to be quite pleasant.

Nina hadn't read Greta the riot act as she'd originally planned when she found her. In fact, they'd only spoken a handful of words to each other since Nina had found them. It seemed Greta knew it was wise to say the least amount possible, until Nina was ready to talk.

Greta lifted the white porcelain teapot and gestured to Nina's cup. "Chamomile, all right?"

Nina nodded. She leaned back in the chair and crossed her arms, watching Greta carefully. "Yeah. It's my favorite actually."

Greta stuck a thin silver spoon in a bear-shaped glass jar of honey and stirred some into her own tea. Nina was surprised at herself that when Greta offered her the jar, she didn't refuse, instead helping herself to a teaspoonful.

"Nina, I have to apologize. What I did was—"

"Greta, I think I judged you a bit harshly—"

Both women had spoken at once, and when Nina laughed at this, Greta did, too. A dam had broken between them.

"You go first, child."

Nina brought the tea to her lips and blew, watching the steam swirl and rise. She reckoned it was odd to have hot tea on a warm day, yet as she sipped, something about the liquid soothed her soul. Chamomile was comfort. It didn't matter the season.

Cradling her teacup, Nina's eyes flicked over Greta. The stern exterior of the woman had definitely been breached. She could see it in the lines of her face and the sadness in her eyes. It almost made her not want to do what she had to do.

"Greta, I think it's time we were honest with each other about our pasts."

The old woman set her lips in a fine line as she fingered the vial at the end of her necklace. "If it'll set your mind at ease, for you, I'll share a bit of my history."

Greta set her teacup down back onto the tray and rose to brace herself against the porch railing. She looked out over the orchard as she spoke. Nina remained in her chair to listen. It seemed Greta needed the space to stir up her ghosts.

"My story is not for the faint of heart, especially not that of a mother's," Greta began. "It was perhaps a little less than half a century ago that things came to a head. But I get ahead of myself.

"When I married Henry, we were so in love. He could do no wrong in my eyes. But after we wed, I saw a different side of him. I spoke to my mother of my concerns, and she assured me that in all marriages, there is an adjustment period. A time of deeper learning of the other person's true nature.

"Henry's nature, I discovered with growing sickness in my heart, was manipulative and vile. He had a constant need to exert his control and establish his dominance. I truly believed that, through acquiescence, docility, and tenderly tending to the hearth as a proper woman should, I could keep his beast at bay.

"A sprinkling of days were joyful, many days monotony, and more days than I care to count were utter agony. I managed, however, all through pregnancy, and all through raising a child. However, when my son grew up and realized my bruises for what they were, my cover stories were no longer able to hide who his father was, and my son challenged Henry's dominance and treatment of me."

Tears dropped between Greta's gnarled fingers. No longer was Nina able to sit by as a witness, the story too much like a twin of her own. She stood and placed her hand over Greta's.

Greta turned, revealing red-rimmed eyes. "Unfortunately, he lost that battle and that day, a part of me was ripped from this earth when my son took his last breath."

It was all Nina could do to keep it together. While a sorrowful sympathy congealed in her veins, the thought of John killing Holden, and leaving her alive to live with what she'd let happen . . . well, it made her want to scream until her throat was raw, to tear away at her flesh until her fingers were knobs and she ceased to exist.

There were no words. Nina knew that the most comforting thing she could offer Greta was her presence. Together, they watched the orchard as crows flew by as apples dislodged themselves from the trees and fell to the ground as puffy white cumulus clouds passed over. Greta straightened again, and Nina followed suit as they returned to the wicker chairs and resumed their tea in silence. Nina topped up their cups with the still-warm water from the pot.

An hour had passed since they'd begun, and Holden's cries now drifted out of the window above like a feather on the wind. He was awake. She bent to carry the tray inside, but Greta shooed her away. "I've got this, child. Go on and tend to your son."

Nina went to the door and stopped halfway through to look back at Greta. "I'd like to take you up on your offer to stay awhile, if you'll have us. At least until we can get back on our feet."

Holding the tea to her lips, Greta offered a warm smile. Now, knowing what she knew, Nina would never be able to unsee the sadness, forever lingering just beneath the surface.

"I would like that," said Greta.

15

The next day, Greta offered to entertain Holden for an hour or two, having unearthed several toys from the attic, including a set of hand-painted wooden alphabet blocks that excited him. Nina took the opportunity to venture back into the orchard, promising to return with fresh apples to finally make the pie for dessert that evening.

Nina kept a brisk pace down to the edge of the trees. Before dipping past the tree line, she turned and took in the sight of the farmhouse perched upon the hill. Against her first impression of the place—dark and imposing— the midday sun offered a new perspective. The intricate woodwork was a lovely pastel yellow that shone softly in the light. For the first time in a long time, she felt hopeful.

She smoothed back her hair, which, for once, she let down in long waves instead of packing it into an untidy bun. She adjusted the basket looped in her arm and stepped past the threshold of the apple trees' open arms. She inhaled, savoring the sweet, ripe scent. Her body vibrated with an unfamiliar nervous energy she couldn't pinpoint. As she wandered through the trees, she realized she'd grown so used to anxiety that it took her some time to identify the feeling of excitement.

Half an hour passed, and she found herself at the four corners of the oldest trees in the orchard yet again. Colin had said he would visit with her today but hadn't mentioned where or how, and this was the only place she thought to search for him. Nina ran her fingers through the leaves and noticed, for the first time, the plump beauty of the red apples hanging from ancient branches so dark they were almost black. Her mouth watered. These apples would be perfect for the pie.

With a reverence she didn't quite understand, Nina opened her palm and cupped an especially enchanting specimen from the tree. As she twisted its stem, something buzzed toward her. Hot pain blossomed from her fingertip. She released the apple, and it fell to the ground as she squinted at the swelling on her forefinger.

A bee sting.

Leaves rustled. Strong hands reached out and embraced her own. It was an effort for Nina to close her gaping mouth as she looked up at Colin, suddenly there, a mixture of ambiguous emotions knitting his brow.

Gently, Colin pinched the tip of the stinger and plucked it from her finger. He held it up for them both to see.

"Such a shame," he said.

"Shame?" Nina pressed her finger to her lips and sucked at it.

Colin stooped and moved aside the apple she'd picked. Nina thought he was going to retrieve it for her. Instead, he searched through the grass until he found what he was looking for: a fuzzy, black-and-yellow-striped body. He lifted it from the ground.

After several seconds of him not making eye contact with her, and only focusing on the dead bee, Nina spoke. "Is something wrong, Colin?"

The anguish on his face seemed to her disproportionate to the death of the insect. "It gave its life to sting you."

"I'm sorry?"

He brusquely marched out toward the old trees and gestured to them. Over his shoulder, he said, "You really shouldn't be picking apples from these trees. Don't you know what they are?"

His lack of concern now for the sting on her finger added an additional sting to her pride.

Nina chewed her fingernail, hating that she felt skittish. "Did I do something to offend you?"

Colin turned to face her, his features softening as he came to her side. "Oh, Nina. Never. It's just that bees are precious few nowadays and important to the orchard. Sorry, I overreacted." He cocked his head in a certain direction. "Come on. I want to show you something."

His seriousness passed away like a cloud. They pushed through the brush to walk through the orchard together. "Where are we going?"

He arched an eyebrow at her mischievously, a charming twinkle in his eyes. "It's a surprise."

It'd been a long while since anyone had given her a good surprise. She played with a button on her dress and admired the view of Colin's backside.

"Okay," she said. "But just so you know, I'm trusting you."

He held her hand as they ducked through a

dense part of the orchard. "I really am sorry for my behavior back there. It must've seemed rather insensitive. The bee colony has been struggling. Each loss could be potentially devastating to the hives."

Nina pressed her hand to her chest, unable to help replaying in her mind the sad, strange song Greta had sung to the bees, by crimson candlelight. "I didn't realize. Greta hadn't mentioned it."

"I don't think she likes to talk about it. Those bees have been passed down from family to family for generations."

"You said something about not picking the apples on those old trees?"

"We're almost there," he said, not answering her.

Sweat gathered at the small of Nina's back. She was amazed at how the walk and the weather didn't even seem to touch Colin. Not a golden hair out of place on that beautiful head of his.

"Those four trees are very special. They were the first four planted at Orchard Hill, one by each member of the original family, Greta's ancestors, and the original settlers of this land. It's very rare for them to still be alive and fruiting." He paused to look back at her. A shadow passed over his face. "It's said that anyone consuming their fruit will forever have a permanent tie to the orchard."

Nina laughed. "Surely, you're joking."

Colin stopped abruptly and stared at her. A smirk broke out on his face, and he elbowed her affectionately. "Of course I'm joking. That's like something out of a fairytale. I wasn't lying about those being original trees, or so Greta has told me. But there is no charm or curse on the apples, my fair Snow White. I just thought it'd be fun to yank your chain."

Nina poked him in the ribs playfully, then lost her balance. He caught her before she fell, their faces inches from each other. She found no flaw in his features this close, and blushed at the slightly absurd notion that he might kiss her.

Colin righted her, yet continued holding her hand and pulled her through into a clearing. A vast field opened up: green swaying grass about knee-high, surrounded by a ring of apple trees. Wild-flowers of all rainbow colors danced in the sun. Fuzzy, pollen-dusted bees flounced from flower to flower. It was an oasis, and she was in awe. Time stood still as Colin led her around.

"It's beautiful," she breathed.

"I like to come here sometimes, to let the rest of the world fall away."

They still held hands. Nina's insides tightened with pleasurable butterflies as she noticed how very alone she was with this handsome stranger. The old Nina never would have dared indulge herself like this.

"You must be very close with Greta, to know so much history about the orchard."

She hated to see his smile falter. He shrugged. "It's hard not to pick up on little facts over time."

Judging by his reaction, she wasn't sure if she should press further, and yet, her curiosity was getting the better of her. When she talked with Greta earlier, it hadn't seemed the time to ask her about what she saw the other night amongst the beehives. Colin may be able to offer insight that Greta wasn't quite ready to share.

"I was wondering if you might help me understand something."

Colin stole her breath away by taking her in his arms. "I'm an open book."

Nina looked down and cleared her throat. "Well, you see, it's not exactly about you, per se. The other night I saw something rather strange out behind the house. I saw Greta with a red candle walking among the beehives. They looked like they were draped with something black, and she was singing. It was the oddest thing."

Nina could've sworn a flash of irritation briefly lit Colin's eyes. He rubbed at his chin and stood back from her. "Huh. I'm not really sure. Have you tried asking Greta?"

Nina deflated. "No, I haven't found the right time. It's really none of my business, anyway." The day's brightness dimmed as the sun sank over the horizon, limning the clouds in lavender and flamingo pink. Nina clucked her tongue against the roof of her mouth. "It's later than I thought it was. I must really be getting back."

Colin smiled sadly. He reached out a hand to her, then let it drop at his side. "Yes, it appears I lose track of the day when I'm with you. I must be going myself."

When they reached the boundaries of the field, he tapped her arm. Nina turned to him with hopeful expectation. The distracted look on his face let her down, and she hoped he didn't notice the blush of embarrassment across her cheeks.

Colin shook his head and swatted at the air as if at an invisible bug. "Are you all right from here? I've got to go this other way and finish up something."

Nina glanced at the darkening path ahead of her and wished she had it in her to ask him to stay. She must remember to ask Greta to borrow a watch so she could keep better track of time. Greta would be needing her help with taking care of Holden and preparing dinner, and she was anxious to return. "Yes, I know the way back from here. See you tomorrow?"

He was already retreating from her, half his face hidden by growing shadows. By some trick of the evening, his voice sounded deeper. "Maybe. If not tomorrow, let's try for sometime this week."

Nina stood there until she could no longer see his blonde hair through the leaves of the trees. She looked down—her basket was still empty. Nina let out a small whine she was reasonably sure Colin wouldn't hear. Casting a frustrated look at the setting sun, Nina trudged forward.

The only way Nina knew how to go back was to pass by the original trees. The sun's only charity was a waning amber light, settling over the crowns of the apple trees. For a second, she let her eyes close, imagining the bright blue of the sky and dark green of the leaves to chase away the trees' more ominous appearance now. A soft fire roared in her belly. She pressed a hand to her torso to quell the irrational emotions. How could she justify being upset with a stranger? Despite only having known him for a day or so, though, Colin didn't *feel* like a stranger to her.

Nina paused, yet again finding herself within the confines of Orchard Hill's four markers of historical significance. She wiped her hands over her face and let out an exasperated sigh. Instead of quelling the anger, it bubbled over within her. She thought she'd found something simple and good with Colin, if only a glimmer.

A crow cackled behind her, causing her to jump. "Shoo!" she yelled, watching it fly away.

She bit her lip and narrowed her eyes at the trees, then began plucking the ruby red apples from the branches, piling them in her basket until it overflowed. Nina grabbed an apple from her basket and brought it to her lips, expecting it to feel more satisfying than it did when she sunk her teeth into it. It was the sweetest bite of apple she'd ever had, far outranking the one from the other night. So sweet, in fact, that it cloyed in her mouth and, as she swallowed, the large piece lodged in her throat.

Nina clawed at her neck and stumbled forward, tripping over something hard that struck her shin. She fell to her hands and knees and flopped onto her back. Her vision swam. The leaves above congealed into a massive blur of reaching hands. Small sounds escaped her mouth, guttural and strangled, not loud enough to carry. No one was coming. She had only herself, and if she didn't do something soon, she would most certainly die.

My fair Snow White.

The irony would've been funny, had she not been turning blue. Nina didn't want to die, not here, not now. Holden was so young. She wanted to be there for him, to witness the man he'd become.

Twice Nina tried to get to her feet, finally managing on the third. She brandished her arms wildly in front of her and aimed for an ashen gray stone protruding from the ground—presumably the object she'd tripped over. Nina was out of time. Her eyes rolled back into her head, and, as she fell forward, she lost consciousness.

The top of the stone caught her in the stomach, and the force of the wind being knocked from her dislodged the apple. Nina coughed up the piece onto the ground and panted for a long time before regaining her breath.

Twisting in the tall grass, Nina looked back at the stone that had first tripped her, then saved her. She clamped her hands over her mouth as she recognized what it was.

A gravestone.

16

S crambling forward, Nina swept aside the grass with a trembling hand, her other clutching her stomach. Stars burst from her lingering dizziness, as the last of the daylight illuminated the mossy head-stone. Every hair on her body prickled.

Here lies Greta Richardson.

Nina didn't stick around to read any more of the inscription. Instead, she snatched up her basket of apples and managed something between a hobble and a run all the way back to the farmhouse, not once looking back over her shoulder. For whatever imaginary frights chased her, a very real one lay ahead. Her sole focus was getting to Holden, and her rational mind couldn't break through the adren-aline pumping through her brain.

Soft light emanated through the farmhouse win-dows, a beacon atop the hill. Nina tripped, recov-ered, and stopped dead in her tracks at the imposing skeletal silhouette waiting for her on the porch.

Greta hurried down the stairs, Holden in tow, and offered her hand to Nina. "My goodness. Are you all right?"

Nina swatted Greta's hand away and took

Holden from her. She squeezed her son tight and stuttered, not sure what to think or say.

"Seriously, child, you look like you've seen a ghost." As Greta took a step near Nina, Nina took a step back.

"That's close enough." Nina held out her palm to stay Greta. "I saw . . . I don't know what I saw. There's a gravestone in the orchard with your name on it."

Greta laughed. Nina frowned harder at her. The older woman's eyebrows arched and the familiar condescending smirk returned. "Nina, really? I know you've had a lot on your mind. But certainly you can't be insinuating what I think you're in-sinuating."

In the porch light, in talking to Greta's very real, very solid form, the idea that the owner of Orchard Hill was somehow a ghost seemed frightfully dumb. "I'm sorry, you're right. It's just that some very odd things have been happening here that I can't ex-plain. I've been having nightmares." Nina scratched her head and swept her hand toward the orchard. "How do you explain the grave?"

Greta raised a slender finger and corrected Nina. "Headstone, not grave. There's nobody buried there."

"What? I don't understand. Why would you do such a thing?"

"You've really got to learn to stop making as-sumptions and listen." Greta went up the porch steps and opened the door, waving Nina and Holden inside. Nina followed Greta into the kitchen, where a nice meal of meat and vegetables awaited them. "Put Holden in his chair and go ahead and start feeding him. I'll be right back."

Nina reluctantly did as instructed. "Where are you going?"

Greta gestured to Nina's knee, scraped and bloodied and coated in dirt. "I'm going to get some things to clean your wound. I'll explain while I tend to it."

They ended up delaying their conversation until after they'd all eaten the food and Nina had put Holden down for the evening. Back in the low-lit kitchen, Nina had her foot propped up while Greta took a damp washcloth to clean out the dirt particles. Nina hissed—two ugly gashes ran parallel across her kneecap, from where she'd run into the stone.

"So you've discovered the ancestral trees."

Nina nodded. "Yes."

"Did you pick these apples from there?"

Greta didn't take her focus off tending to Nina's knee, and her face was unreadable.

"I did," Nina said, guilt seeping into her tone.

"Good. It's tradition that only family should eat from those trees." Greta paused and tenderly placed a hand on Nina's shoulder. In that moment, they were kindred spirits again. "I know you're not blood, child. But I hope it's okay if I've come to think of you and that sweet little boy as family. Besides, it seems like you could use a little family right now."

Nina's eyes stung with tears. She knew if she started crying now, she may not stop. She dipped her head at Greta in a heartfelt thank you. "Even after how I've treated you?"

The old woman smiled. "Even after. Besides, I'd be surprised if a scare like that didn't make you a little jumpy." Greta winked at her and stood, cracking her back as she straightened. "Right, let's get started on that pie, and I'll tell you how there came to be a headstone on my property with my name on it."

The oven ticked when Greta hit the button to warm it up, the natural gas kicking on. "You know how to make apple pie from scratch?"

Nina shook her head as she washed the apples in the sink and set them on a hand towel to dry.

"Would you like to learn?" Greta asked.

The night was jet black, the bee boxes visible in the moonlight through the kitchen window. Nina chewed the inside of her cheek and wondered whether Greta's kindness came from seeing herself in Nina, or if she actually liked Nina herself. This was her chance to get to know the older woman better.

Nina joined Greta at the kitchen island, where she was spreading flour on the well-worn, oak surface.

As Nina got to work on the crust, Greta peeled and chopped the apples. The oven flared again, and Greta began to talk. "That headstone saved my life."

A measure of silence followed, so long that Nina was tempted to encourage her to continue.

"After my son was killed." Another pause accompanied an audible swallow. "Everyone believed Henry when he said it was an accident. The three of us alone out here on the farm . . . There was no one to believe my word over his. Whenever I tried to tell anyone, they dismissed me as a distraught mother, telling me that I was using it as an explanation for what was just a sad random occurrence." She snorted. "Some even tried to give me that bull about God calling home an angel early."

"I can't imagine . . ." Though that wasn't wholly

true—Nina didn't know what it was like to lose a child, yet she was certainly familiar with no one believing her against her husband's word.

Greta cleared her throat. Her chopping became sterner. "Right. After Henry died, everyone suspected foul play on my part. However, the sheriff found no evidence or reason to suspect me when the coroner deduced Henry died of anaphylactic shock, as a result of bee stings. I buried my wretched husband in the town cemetery, and when I returned home that day, that headstone was leaning against the front door.

"Some town joke or threat, whatever—I got the message that I was no longer all that welcome in town. However, the damn thing was so heavy I had to go in and out the back door, and no one would help me move it. They even started rumors about me being cursed or some such nonsense.

"Day after day, the presence of the thing grated on me, and loneliness spread its roots within me. One day, it wasn't more special than any other, mind you, except for perhaps the conditions—the angle of the sun, the wind in the air, reminded me of the day my son passed.

"It wasn't the first time the thought occurred to me. It was the first time I intended to act upon it." Greta set the knife down on the cutting board and bowed her head. Nina hated seeing such an otherwise normally poised woman in a state like this.

"I intended to do it right there at the old trees, thinking I could return to my family that way somehow. Be a part of the orchard forever." Greta pushed away from the kitchen island and moved over to stand at the sink, gazing out of the window at the hives. "When I got there, the sun beamed so bright it was blinding, like a spotlight on my headstone. I had no idea how it could've gotten there, or how anyone would've known what I was going to do. I hardly knew it myself until I was walking there.

"As I kneeled in front of my own grave, I wanted to pray. I even clasped my hands together in prayer." Greta banged her hands against the porcelain with a dull clang. "But how could I reach out to a God who would let my baby be taken from me?" Greta's voice broke, and her next words were barely audible. "How could I ask for forgiveness if I couldn't forgive myself?"

Withdrawing a handkerchief from her pocket, Greta dabbed at the tears on her face. "As I kneeled that day in the orchard at the foot of my own grave, I swear I saw my son. I think he was telling me to stay. So I stayed, and even if I can't forgive myself, I hope he forgives me."

Nina joined Greta, looking out behind Orchard Hill farmhouse and placed a hand on Greta's back. In silence, out of an unspoken respect for the past and the dead, they finished making the pie and put it in the oven.

While the feel-good smells of butter, sugar, and apples filled the air in the house, chasing away awful memories, Nina brewed some tea, and they sat together out in the wicker chairs on the front porch.

"This is becoming a nice ritual for us, isn't it?" Greta asked. Nina could count on one hand the amount of times Greta had asked a simple, pleasant question, one that didn't make her question her entire life.

Nina smiled into the comforting warmth of her chamomile. "It is." They listened to the music of the crickets and watched fireflies prickle the orchard with their tiny lights. "I met your farmhand, by the way. He's an . . . odd fellow. Strange, but sweet." She blushed.

Greta took a long sip of her tea, her gaze distant. "Come again, child?"

Nina fumbled with her tea. "Oh, I was just saying that I met Colin. He's quite handsome. All the girls in town must find him quite charming."

Greta clicked her tongue against her teeth and was silent for some time, staring out into the dark.

"Did I say something wrong?" Nina asked.

The old woman stirred, waving her hand dismissively. "Of course not. It's just been a long day." She sat forward. "But Nina, be careful with him. He's not . . . right for you. Especially not now, considering all you're going through."

Nina mouthed an *oh*. She leaned back in her chair and avoided Greta's eyes. Who was she to tell Nina who was and wasn't right for her? Shouldn't she, better than anyone else, know what having a good man in her life would mean to her?

She refreshed her tea, adding an extra helping of honey. Wanting to talk about anything else, Nina spoke. "Greta, I hope it's not too trying to ask—the other night I saw you with the candle among the beehives?"

Greta stirred her tea and nodded. "Haven't you ever heard of telling the bees, child?"

Child—this was starting to signify that there was a lesson to be learned. Nina was pleased to find she didn't read condescension into the word, whether because they were growing closer, or because it was never truly there to begin with.

Nina shook her head. "I'm pretty much a suburban girl. A lot of the stuff on the orchard is new to me."

"You don't give yourself enough credit." Greta relaxed into the back of the wicker chair with a soft creak. "I suppose it isn't a very common tradition nowadays. These bees have been in my family for generations. They keep the orchard thriving, and therefore, they've kept my family alive. It's only proper that when one of us dies, we pay our respects."

Nina's eyes widened. "Did someone die recently?"

Greta patted Nina's hand. "Don't worry. I'm the last of my line. When my son died, Henry deemed the tradition a fool's errand, a silly superstition. He denied me my right to tell the bees my baby was gone. So, every night, since the headstone, I sing to them of our loss. But I fear it's too late."

Nina leaned forward, her elbows on her knees. "What's too late?"

Greta set her tea down. A haggardness was evident in her face, accentuating her true age. She brushed back a strand of peppered hair and stared out into the darkness of the orchard.

"The bees are dying," she whispered.

17

Weeks flew by, summer aging rapidly, autumn nipping at its heels. The air had cooled to a bearable temperature and was bordering on pleasant. The trees even took on a nice, gilded hue.

Nina had asked if she could be Greta's 'beekeeping apprentice.' She had no illusions that she would learn enough to help save the bees, but she could tell Greta needed someone there with her, as each day they found more little bodies no longer buzzing. Not even the newer hive they'd discovered in the attic helped much.

Learning beekeeping was slow going. Greta talked Nina through everything over their morning tea on the porch, and then Greta would stay in the house and watch Holden while Nina suited up and worked out back. Never in her life would she have thought she'd enjoy the hard work involved with maintaining beehives. Yet she took quite a liking to it, along with the satisfying simplicity of other tasks around Orchard Hill. Cleaning up the house, sprucing up the garden, cooking with Greta, playing with Holden—Nina relaxed into the forward momentum of structured days and even slept well at

night, falling asleep to the soft snores of her
little boy.

Peaceful days passed into those quiet summer
nights. More and more, Nina found herself wanting
to stay. Greta made good on her promise to pay Nina
each week, and even opened a fresh bank account
for Nina. The money had accumulated such that
Nina probably could move on, but with each sign of
the beehives' impending death, Greta appeared
frailer, and Nina couldn't bear to leave the old
woman alone. Besides, with Greta making weekly
trips into town for groceries, Nina didn't need to
leave. She was starting to feel safe at the farmhouse.

There were other reasons to stay, as well. In rare
moments, when she didn't have any responsibilities
and Greta felt up to watching Holden, Nina stole
away to spend time with Colin. His strange behavior
that one day had proved an anomaly, and increas-
ingly she found herself feeling free and tranquil
with him, enjoying easy conversation and genuine
laughter, her worries scattered away like dandelion
seeds on the wind.

Today, she met him in what she'd come to think
of as "their field." Over one arm, she carried a
checkered blanket and picnic basket brimming with
treats she'd made herself. Once she located a patch
relatively clear of high grasses and blossoms, Nina
settled in and waited. His timing was always im-
peccable.

Through the wildflowers, she watched him
walking toward her, the sunlight making his blonde
hair something of a golden halo. He wore his stan-
dard attire, a loose-buttoned cotton shirt and dark
denim jeans. A blush crept up her neck as he approached her.

"For someone who claims to do maintenance around an orchard, you sure never seem to break a sweat." Nina brushed back her hair, hoping the gesture came off more casual than nervous. She'd decided that today was the day she'd try to get a little closer to Colin.

Colin flopped down on the blanket beside her. He crossed his legs and propped his elbows to lean closer to her. "Are you saying you'd like to see me sweat?"

Nina was all but struck mute. Whereas she'd trotted over to the field bravely, on a mission, all such fiery courage now drained away under his penetrating gaze. She licked her lips when he didn't falter. She felt like they were caught in a game of chicken, and wanted to kick herself when she turned away first.

"What did you bring today?" Colin nudged open the lid of the picnic basket with his finger.

"Blackberry tarts. I picked them myself," she said proudly.

Colin slipped his hand inside the basket and withdrew a tart. He feigned a bite. Then, he offered it to Nina. She laughed and took a tentative nibble.

"Come on, you can do better than that." His other hand rested on her thigh, and she took a sizable bite of the tart. An involuntary moan escaped her lips as she chewed. Her cheeks went red.

Nina wiped the crumbs at the corner of her mouth. "Sorry," she mumbled.

Colin cupped her face with his hand. "You've got nothing to be sorry for."

She allowed herself to nuzzle her cheek in his palm, to smell the nectar-sweet musk of his skin.

Mere inches from each other, Nina embraced her opportunity and leaned forward for a kiss.

Her attempt was met with—nothing. She opened her eyes, startled to see Colin was no longer beside her. He stood facing away, his body rigid with a tension she couldn't understand.

"Nina," he said. "I can't tell you how much our time together has meant to me. But there's something I have to tell you."

Nina rose to her feet and went to him, feeling an overwhelming need to drive away the sadness in his voice. "I think I know what you're going to say." How could she ever have been so bold as to assume that he was free? True, he'd never mentioned anyone else. And yet, she knew someone so kind and beautiful must be spoken for. What else could explain this change in him? "But we haven't done anything improper yet." Her words came out in a rush. She went to embrace him and then dropped her arms to her side. "It's such a perfect day. Can we just have this time together, and you can tell me next time?"

Colin looked down at her and smiled. She longed to brush away the grimness underneath. "I don't see the harm in that."

The air was pregnant with unsaid words. Nina jabbed him in the ribs with her elbow and grabbed a long stick off the ground. "Come on, want to show me that move you did when we first met?"

He arched an eyebrow and flashed a grin at her. "And what move was that?"

She leveled the stick at him like a rifle. Before she knew it, he closed the distance between them, snatching the stick away from her and affectionately pushing her to the ground.

As they both laughed, Colin helped her up. In

their breathless momentum, her body pressed almost magnetically against his, and their lips found one another, and they kissed. Everywhere his body touched hers, her skin vibrated with excitement and desire. Her hands on his strong biceps, his hands stroking her lower back, their hips against one another, her breasts pressed against his chest. His tongue danced with hers. He tasted sweet, like apples.

As quickly as she sank into him, savoring the sweetness of his lips and inhaling the mesmerizing scent of his musky cologne, she tugged away. Her hand rested firmly on his chest, outstretched to keep them apart. She licked her lips. It did nothing to subdue the fire blazing across her body.

Nina cast her eyes downward. If she looked into his eyes, gray as luminescent storm clouds, she wouldn't be able to contain herself. "I'm so sorry. You'll have to forgive me."

Colin laid a hand on hers, keeping her in touch with his chest. "It is I who should ask for your forgiveness. You have no idea—"

Breaking through the brush, a faun and its mother leaped into the field and paused. Nina and Colin locked eyes with the deer and doe, the four held almost in a trance.

Crows burst through the trees with their rough calls, startling away the deer. Nina withdrew her hand from Colin, shaking her head many times over. "I really must be going. I've been gone far too long. Greta and Holden will be needing me. We can talk about this later."

She took off a couple of steps too far, now committed to not looking back. Nina figured she could retrieve the blanket and basket later. Nothing in her wanted to hear Colin's next words—that he had a girlfriend, or worse, a wife. She didn't want to break the spell. Yet it seemed that, no matter how long she tried to put it off, outside forces were conspiring to ruin her sanctuary.

18

When Nina came downstairs into the kitchen the next morning, Holden on her hip, Greta was at the table, scooping papers into a faded manila folder.

"Breakfast is in the oven," Greta said. "I have to go into town for a bit to handle some paperwork. I should be back by lunch."

Nina peeked in the oven window, even though she had an inkling of the delight it contained. "Wow, cinnamon rolls. What did we do to deserve this special treatment?"

Greta finished packing her purse and shoved the folder under her arm. "Nothing in particular. Just keeping an old woman company in her winter years is enough, my lovelies." With a peck on the cheek for Holden and a nod to Nina, Greta was out the door.

After retrieving the buns from the oven, Nina sat down to her meal. She broke off tiny bits of the gooey pastry for Holden. She'd not fed him such sweet treats, and it was a joy to see such light in his eyes. "I'm gonna regret this, aren't I?"

She wiggled her eyebrows up and down in an exaggerated manner, and Holden giggled. Nina thoroughly savored a chance to spend some quality time alone with Holden in the farmhouse. It also gave her an excuse not to go out searching for Colin.

She wiped down Holden's sticky fingers with a wet washcloth and set him down to explore. Away from the hustle and bustle of the suburban world, she marveled at how much easier it was to be present in the moment, to enjoy being with her son. The way he lit up as she smiled when he pointed at a bird out the window or watching him try to squat and balance as he inspected his toys on the floor—it was a simple joy.

The moments rushed by too quickly, even as she tried to soak up every one. Every day, his face changed, maturing, becoming a little leaner. He was losing his baby fat, looking more and more like a toddler. Did all parents love their children so fiercely? The idea of that much sheer love in the world was more than she could comprehend. Part of her felt a pang of guilt at denying John these precious moments. But if he loved Holden as much as she did, he sure had a hell of a way of showing it.

A car door slammed. Nina looked at the clock. It was only ten in the morning. As Nina lifted aside the curtain to see out front, she chattered to Holden, the way she narrated everything she could to him. "What's Greta doing back so early?"

Peering through their gauzy cloth, she saw it wasn't the familiar truck but rather a sheriff's four-door sedan. Her heart thumped in her chest. She released the curtains and stepped behind the window frame.

From what she could still see, a tall, broad man with a thick white mustache exited the vehicle. He adjusted his utility belt. Nina's pulse raced faster. She retreated from the window and scooped up Holden. She'd only just backed against the far wall into the shadows when the man's silhouette darkened the window, and he cupped his hand to the glass.

After a long pause, the sheriff moved to the door. Nina could almost time the knock by the familiar creaks of the porch boards. Halfway up the staircase —when the knock came—she prayed he wouldn't see her through the foyer windows as she skulked her way to the landing.

"Hello? Anybody home?" The sheriff had exactly the kind of gruff voice she'd expect. She'd met plenty of John's police colleagues at barbecues and gatherings.

Miraculously, Holden hadn't cried or screamed. *Yet.* She figured the safest thing to do would be to get them to the attic before the sheriff heard them. She was almost to the second landing when she heard the slam of another car door.

Nina scampered the rest of the way to the attic, set Holden down, and shut the door. She rushed over to the windows facing the front of the house and teased one open, half an inch. From this angle, she could only see Greta's truck, and assumed Greta was talking to the sheriff on the front porch.

The wind muffled their conversation. Nina only caught every couple of words: "Do you know . . . Missing . . . Husband beside himself . . ."

Nina covered her mouth and eased the window closed. She pressed her back against the wall and slid to the floor, wrapping her arms around her knees. Holden waddled over to her and gave her a big hug and open-mouthed kiss. Nina held him close and rocked him until he squirmed away to explore once more. She prayed Greta would be convincing enough to make the sheriff go away.

19

A soft rap on the attic door stirred Nina from her crouching position. She assumed Holden would've pestered her to play before Greta found them, and when she lifted her head to an empty room, her breath sped, and her heart beat loudly in her ears.

"Nina? Are you in there?" Greta called from the other side of the door.

Nina ignored Greta's approaching footsteps as she frantically searched the room for her son. "Holden?"

A bony hand clamped her shoulder. "Didn't you hear me? I was calling to you. I've been worried." Greta was out of breath, and her hair, usually well-kempt, was frazzled.

"I can't find him," Nina said. She continued darting around the room "He was right here, and the door was closed. He couldn't have gotten out, could he?"

Greta's eyes widened. Then she planted herself in front of Nina and caught her by the arms. "Shhhh."

Nina struggled against her. "What are you doing? I have to—"

Greta raised a talon-like finger in the air. "Listen, child."

Forcing an exaggerated sigh, Nina tried to relax her shoulders and do as the woman suggested. Her heart stopped, and the blood in her veins turned to sludge as she waited. Greta's grip was strong on her upper arms, warning her to stay still.

A rustling noise, followed by a giggle, alerted them.

"Holden!" Nina cried and slid over next to a cardboard box. Holden was inside, playing with a smattering of well-worn baby toys. Nina picked him up and hugged him tight. His tiny hand gripped the corner of a satin, pastel-yellow baby blanket. Tears leaked from her eyes as she held him close, her blood circulating again now that she'd found him. Nina had been holding her breath far too long. It caught in her throat as she inhaled deeply.

She bit her bottom lip. "We can't stay here any longer, can we?"

The muscles in Greta's jaw worked, and she crossed her arms. "I gather you two were up here hiding from Sheriff Wesson, then?"

Nina nodded. She half-expected Greta to spit on the floor after saying the sheriff's name. But then, of course, Greta was not the sort of woman taken to doing something so undignified as spitting.

Greta led Nina and Holden toward the attic door and down the stairs. "Don't you worry about him. He's been giving me trouble for years. Wesson's father and Henry were right good friends. And the apple didn't fall far from *that* particular tree, if that tells you something about the sheriff."

Nina's mouth puckered as if she'd taken a swig of sour milk. *The apple didn't fall far from the tree.* What a terrible old saying. She kissed Holden's soft cheek and did her best to ignore how much he looked like John. "So, Wesson wasn't here for us?" Nina adjusted Holden to the other hip. He delighted in rubbing the soft fabric of his baby blanket on his face, which coaxed a low-spirited smile from her.

"Oh, he sure was. But that husband of yours doesn't own you, and you have every right to be here."

Nina wasn't sure how much more stress her heart could take. She was also fully aware that John would exploit every legal angle he could to get them back. And when it came to Holden—well, she wasn't exactly square legally, was she?

"Greta, please tell me you didn't tell him I'm here."

The woman whirled through the swinging kitchen door with a graceful flourish only she could pull off, then held it for Nina. "After our time together, I would've thought you knew me better than that." The corners of Greta's lips curved upward in a knowing smile as if they shared an amusing secret. Nina supposed they did. However, she would've described it as anything but amusing.

Nina collapsed into one of the kitchen island chairs and let Holden down to wander. She leaned back and pressed her hand to her chest. "Oh, thank goodness." Unable to settle into a comfortable position, Nina sat forward and hung her head in her hands. "Greta, I've got to tell you something I should've told you awhile back."

From the stovetop, Greta retrieved the cast-iron teakettle, decorated with dancing bees and dainty honeycombs, and filled it with water from the sink. The last of the backyard sun twinkled through the queen bee vial that hung from her necklace like a suncatcher. "What's that?"

Nina rubbed her forefingers to her temples. "John's a cop."

Greta straightened at the stovetop, where she set the kettle back on the burner. Nina winced, expecting the worst—outrage, scolding, banishment. After a heavy measure of silence, Greta shrugged. "Let them try to take you and that sweet boy from here." She used her chin to gesture at Holden. "Cop or no, I'm not going to let them hurt you anymore."

Nina sighed. It was perhaps the sweetest sentiment anyone had shown her. Unfortunately, as a woman well into her eighties, Greta was growing feebler by the day. No matter how stern Greta could be, John was strong and not afraid to use it, especially against those less able.

Busying herself, Nina started setting the tea tray with saucers and cups. "I can't thank you enough for the haven you've provided for me and my son, Greta. But I can't put you in danger any longer. I'll pack up tonight and, if tomorrow morning you can drop us in the next town or two over, we'll be on our way."

Perched at the kitchen sink, Greta slammed the porcelain with her palms. It was a move that Nina was beginning to realize comforted Greta as the old woman looked out over her beehives. "I refuse to accept that. You've made a home here. You seem happy here. Holden seems happy here. If you run now, you might never stop running—"

A loud *smack* in the corner of the kitchen alerted Nina. Holden began howling in pain. Nina hurried across the tile and inspected him. He was already smiling and laughing again. Still, she double-checked to make sure the redness on his forehead was nothing but a surface wound.

It never ceased to amaze her how many times a toddler could fall and get back up like nothing happened. It also amazed her how it added another gray hair to her head every single time. To have a child was to live with a part of yourself outside your body, vulnerable and precious. Nina wrapped her arms around her little boy and peered up at Greta, wishing she knew the right move. Because, perhaps, in this case, there was the *right* thing to do and the *safe* thing to do.

Her hesitation must've shown, as Greta opened her mouth, likely so she could convince Nina to stay. Remaining crouched next to Holden, Nina fetched the baby blanket from the floor, which seemed to be the culprit for Holden's fall.

"Let me take that," Greta said, swiftly removing the blanket from Nina's grasp. "I didn't realize Holden had taken this tatty old thing from the attic."

Holden screamed and reached for the blanket, tugging down a corner. Nina was puzzled by Greta's harshness, but assumed it must've belonged to her son. As she pried Holden's hands from the fabric, Nina spotted embroidered lettering underneath his fingers. She spread it out to read it fully. An abrupt static in Nina's ears drowned out any of Greta's words. Her body went numb.

Colin, it read.

She remembered something she'd once dismissed: the *G + C* inscribed on the ancient tree. She'd brushed it off as someone Greta had perhaps had an affair with during her unhappy marriage. Now Nina saw it in a new light—as a love note from

Greta to her child, forever binding them in spirit on that ancestral bark.

Nina's fingers trembled, her mouth went dry. Nina always assumed that Greta's son was fairly young when he died. Then it occurred to her she'd only assumed that because her own son was so young. To challenge his father, the boy must've been older and stronger.

Still unable to hear anything but her own words, Nina spoke. "How old was your son when he died?"

"What?" Greta pressed a hand to her chest, apparently taken aback by the question.

Nina rose to face Greta and repeated herself. "It's important. How old was your son when he died?"

Greta's tough exterior looked poised to crumble. She huffed, straightened her shoulders, and clasped the vial on her chain, like it was some sort of protective amulet. "He was twenty-seven. Why should that matter?"

Nina squeezed her nails into her palms, until redness swelled in half-moon cuts. "This is his blanket?" Nina held it up to Greta, who shied away from it as if it could sting her. She couldn't hide the accusatory tone from her voice. "You never mentioned his name."

"I don't like to say it." Greta's lips were firm, her eyes steely, defiant.

The teakettle whistled loudly, screaming between them until Nina blinked. Greta didn't say a word as she removed it from the stove and prepared their tea. Yet Nina could tell by the extra stiffness in the woman's shoulders that she'd upset her.

Nina wanted nothing more in the world than to refuse to believe the evidence staring her in the face. It would have to be the most miraculous coincidence on record if there just happened to be a farm-hand with the same age and name hanging around Orchard Hill. A man she'd been spending so much time with, a man she'd grown very fond of, a man that she might even—

The word emerged full formed from the mists of her mind, refusing to leave until she confronted it. Because if it was not a coincidence, then Colin was a—

Ghost, her mind answered her.

20

Nina lay Holden in the crib in the guest room
and stroked the bridge of his nose. Nestled
under one arm was Stego and, under the other, the
satin blanket, compelling her to read the name over
and over—*Colin, Colin, Colin*. It was like a phone
ringing off the hook, relentless until she answered it.
She'd tried to take the blanket away from Holden,
thinking it would be morbid for him to have it,
though her heart didn't quite agree. Either way,
Holden screamed and screamed, hot tears spilling
down his cheeks until she let him have it.

She tiptoed down the hall to Greta's room,
which Nina had never visited before. Compared to
the rest of the farmhouse, the décor was strikingly
spare. A single bed marked the center of the room,
and a vanity, with hardly any knickknacks, stood
flush against the interior wall. Sheer maple curtains
dressed the windows, and two floor lamps rose at
attention on either side of the bed. A hope chest
rested at the foot of the bed, open and overflowing
with sepia photos and albums—a vessel containing
Orchard Hill's memories. It dawned on Nina that

the house was not decorated with pictures of the family, something that had always niggled at the back of her mind. Now she knew why.

Nina stood in the doorway, giving Greta some space. The woman sat perched over a large album with brown leather binding, Polaroids neatly tucked into the clear plastic sleeves. Greta appeared haggard, unlike her normal state, where she held her age at bay from her face. Her complexion was ashen, making the red of her lipstick stand out like a smear of blood. On the floor, indentations marked the wood where a much bigger bed used to be. Greta had apparently cleared out the room and hidden any memory of Henry, but it also seemed to extend to Colin.

Nina tapped her knuckles softly on the door and offered a sympathetic look to Greta. "May I?"

Greta patted the quilt on the bed next to her. Outside, the sun was setting, its glow a milk-choco-latey cream through the curtains. Nina flicked on one of the floor lamps before taking her seat next to Greta.

The old woman, who smelled soothingly of rosemary and honey, ran her time-ravaged fingers over a photo of a mother and baby, newly born and snuggled close to her breast. The aquiline nose of the much younger woman, nestled in the downy golden hair of the babe, left no doubt who it was.

As if reading Nina's mind, Greta asked, "Where does the time go?"

Nina saw herself in the future as an old woman, knowing that, in the blink of an eye, she would be in Greta's place. It was an ache born within her chest the day her son came into the world. She thought of something her mother used to say.

There but for the grace of God go I.

Tears gathered in the corners of her eyes. Nina wrapped her arms around the woman as Greta lovingly flipped through the album. Together they watched through the yellowing photos, a young boy growing into a man and a woman doing her best to raise him well.

"It seems like there were some good times?" Nina ventured, treading carefully.

Greta tapped a photo, crookedly taken with half of Greta's younger face captured and the big, broad smile of what looked to be a young Colin, maybe eight years old. "Look at me, taking a selfie before it was the thing to do."

The women chuckled together, then fell into a somber silence. Greta sighed. "He was just on the brink of starting his life. He'd come back to help out here at Orchard Hill. I'd hoped he'd meet some nice girl in town and settle down, prayed he'd turn out nothing like his father."

Greta stood and filed through the hope chest, zeroing in on a particular album, and brought it over to show Nina. She flipped to a page and pointed to it.

Nina's blood ran cold. Suspecting was one thing; confirmation was quite another. Greta's son was indeed her Colin, from the golden halo of hair to the smirk in his smile and the arch of his brow. Nina looked at Greta. The family resemblance in the facial expression hit her like a ton of bricks.

"You don't have to say it," Greta said. "I've suspected for years. You seeing him confirms it."

"What?" Nina squeaked. It wasn't enough of a question for the implications, and yet, it was all Nina could offer from her suddenly parched throat.

"I wasn't fully honest with you about Henry's death." Greta grasped the vial with the bee inside, letting it rattle against the glass and holding it up to the lamplight. She let it fall back against her clavicle, then rose to face the antique mirror atop the vanity, speaking to their reflections. "As I told you, after . . . you know. Being alone with Henry in this house, filled with so many memories of our son, I was in a dark place. Henry wouldn't let me grieve.

"My mother and my mother's mother had always impressed upon me the importance of telling the bees of family members' deaths. The first day after I buried my son, the bees began to act strangely. As you know, I tend to them frequently, and at first, I figured they missed my presence. Bees are actually more intuitive than you think. They can even recognize different people.

"A week later, the bees pelted themselves against the windows. Further burying me in my turmoil, it pained me greatly to find their little bodies fallen outside the kitchen window. I knew they were in search of me and wondering where Colin was. I pleaded with Henry, injuring my pride—whatever pride could've possibly have even remained—begging on hands and knees for him to allow me this one reprieve from my grief. And still he denied me, even going to great lengths to lock me in the house.

"Then, I tried reason—explaining to him how, if the bees all died, that Orchard Hill would go right along with it. The orchard was our livelihood."

Greta flinched. "He spat in my face and told me it would be what I deserved, for failing as a mother, for raising a boy who would lift his hand to his father.

"My thoughts turned murderous. I vowed my

last act would be in defiance of this man who'd ripped everything away from me. A man so small and jealous he couldn't allow me one ounce of happiness in this world."

Greta reached up and released her hair from its pin, allowing the dark-gray-and-silver hair to cascade freely, hiding her face in shadow. "In the middle of the night, I crept up to the attic and winched open one of the windows." She again held up her vial; with the movement, it seemed like the bee moved of its own accord. "I swear, this very honeybee waited for me outside that window. I sang a mournful, venomous song, telling the only creatures in the world who would believe me of how my husband killed my son.

"That morning, when Henry found me curled in the attic in nothing but my nightgown and slippers, my tears and emotions spent until I was a husk of myself, he dragged me downstairs and out into the middle of the bee boxes. He proceeded to beat me like never before. Usually, he delivered blows punctuated by 'lessons' that I should learn, if I wanted to stay a good wife. This time, there were no lessons.

"I was surely within an inch of my life, my vision swelling shut, my consciousness fading."

Greta clutched her chest. Tears stained the vanity's woodgrain. Nina raised an involuntary hand to her eye, knowing all too well how close she'd come to a similar fate.

"Through my dim vision, I witnessed every single bee rise into the sky like a flight of tiny angels from those hives. I've never seen anything like it. They swarmed in a tornado of wrath, encasing Henry, their wings vibrating with fury—a black mass avenging my son and protecting me.

"The papers failed to mention the beating, or how I was in the hospital for weeks after. No, they mourned a 'beloved' figure of this stupid little town, and pointed fingers at me.

"Colin . . . I didn't want to hope. I didn't want to believe that it was him."

Greta shook her head. Her waves of streaked hair shivered like fine silk. "However, seeing my son at my headstone, by the ancestral trees, and swearing I caught glimpses of his blonde hair wandering the orchard over these long years, it's difficult to deny the weight of his presence at Orchard Hill. I sing to the bees in hopes that he'll forgive me. I want him to find peace. This life, holding onto the anger and poison of the past, I wouldn't wish it upon anyone, least of all my only son. I almost wish I'd never sang to the bees that night—"

Nina raised her head and locked eyes with Greta through the mirror. "Don't say that. He saved your life."

"A life racked with loneliness, guilt, and regret? It would've been a mercy to let me die that day."

Exhaustion overcame Nina. She longed to retreat to the guest room and curl up in her bed, to reach her hands through the slats of Holden's crib and sleep with her hand on her son's back. She embraced Greta in a long hug and wished her good night, promising they'd speak more about this tomorrow . . . and figure out what to do.

What to do? Nothing clear came to mind.

As Nina shed her clothes from the day and pulled on cool linen pajamas, she crawled into bed and turned out the light.

In the dark, a thought disturbed her: Greta had a point. If Colin could show himself to Nina, why not give Greta that same comfort? It was hard not to conclude that he might've done so out of an attempt to punish his mother for failing to protect him.

Sorrow and fatigue washed over her. It wasn't long before she fell into a fitful sleep.

21

That night, Nina dreamed of walls that seeped warm, golden-brown honey, and a farmhouse that whispered her name. Unable to sleep, she rose before Holden awoke and quickly dressed. As soon as he was up, she changed his diaper, and they went down to the front porch, where Greta had already set up their usual morning tea.

Anxious, Nina handed Holden to Greta. "Are you able to watch him this morning? There's something I've gotta do."

Greta raised her eyebrows but didn't question. "Of course."

When Nina reached the bottom of the porch steps, she halted and turned. "I'm curious, Greta. Where was Colin buried?" She had a feeling, of course, she already knew.

This question put a small, wicked grin on Greta's face. "I suppose that is one victory I had over Henry." She let Holden down to sit next to her on the porch and steepled her fingers. "The funeral director happens to be an old family friend. After some convincing," Greta rubbed her fingers together to indicate cash, "she agreed to pretend to bury Colin in the town cemetery but, instead, held a private ceremony with me to bury him in his favorite place in the orchard."

"The wildflower field in the back of the orchard. Right?"

Greta dipped her head. "If you find him, tell him I'm—"

"I will." Nina nodded solemnly, then raced off into the orchard, avoiding the ancient trees with Greta's headstone. She didn't need to pass through that morose landmark today, and by now, she knew the orchard like the back of her hand.

Spotlights of reds, oranges, and magentas appeared as the sun poked up over the horizon. Nina stopped to catch her breath at the edge of the clearing. Summer blossoms freckled the field, welcoming with their pleasing fragrance. She scanned the grasses for any movement but saw none, not even the usual squirrels or odd rabbit.

As she listened, silence crept upon her as the chirping crickets and babbling birds hushed all at once, as if out of grim respect.

Now, more than ever, when Nina crossed the grassy threshold into the field, she felt like she was entering a different world. Her ears popped faintly, as they did at high elevations, or on planes. The air was that perfect mix of cool and fresh, leaving her with a surreal weightlessness. She caressed the flowers as she walked through them, leaving them bobbing in her wake.

Drawn to the center of the flowered field, from which she detected a faint buzzing sound, Nina took a path that was not wholly at her whim. She treaded with care toward a dense, oblong patch of lilies here that she'd never noticed before. Perhaps they'd only recently bloomed since the last time she visited with Colin.

Liquid gold sunlight poured over her and the field, highlighting every drop of dew and petal in breathtaking detail. A sense of dread grew in her stomach as she neared her destination. The air had taken on a molasses quality, as if the closer she got, the more time slowed, until it threatened to stand still entirely. She closed her eyes. The half-hearted breeze sifted through her hair and smelled of the coming fall on the wind—ripe apples, turning leaves, a hint of death.

Nina wrinkled her nose. It might be true, that the coming of autumn signaled something like a death, but she was fairly certain this might be the actual *scent* of death. She sure as hell knew what fresh death smelled like—John had seen to that. He'd bring home glassy-eyed deer in the back of his truck, the head flopping at a grisly angle, bragging about his kill and how he'd bagged the best buck of the day among his hunting buddies.

Nina rubbed her upper arms and shivered. Bile singed the lining of her esophagus, and Nina had to breathe steadily through her mouth to keep it at bay. No, this death smelled much, *much* older than that. It reminded her faintly of a dead rat she'd once found in a trap in the basement. She'd meant to check and replace the traps monthly, as she always had, but after giving birth to Holden, it had slipped her mind for many months. When she finally got around to checking them, the rat had long since shriveled to a mummy of itself, each slender bone visible through its emaciated, dull black fur.

Nina marched closer as her heart knocked against her ribs, urging her to turn back. Her legs refused to listen and carried her forward, as if in a trance. She stared hard at the patch of orange flowers which rimmed the outline of the oblong formation. The innermost flowers were laden with bees, black swarming masses coating every inch of the petals, their drone almost deafening.

She blinked several times. The tiger-striped heads of the lilies were like cups overflowing, the bees too heavy for their lanky stems to support. Where the petals once praised the sky, the flowers now bowed under the weight of bustling yellow-black bodies. The tips of Nina's fingers went numb, and her skin tingled.

Even if this were a natural occurrence, she would've expected the flowers to droop this way and that, not in a specific direction, not forming the sharp outline of a man. The flowers were so tall she couldn't see what lay inside until she was nearly on top of the phenomenon. Nina inched forward and thought her eardrums would surely burst at the buzz.

Inside the man-shaped flower outline, bees danced in flits and flashes over something alarmingly white and disturbingly familiar. She gasped, a strangled, awful sound escaping her throat, her mind making quick work of the puzzle before her. Responding to her exclamation like it was a command, the bees flushed away from the uppermost portion, revealing the skull's eternal grimace on its fleshless head.

Nina screamed. In unison, the bees erupted into the air, a vibrating beast hovering above its charge. The bone-chilling picture of what lay within the tomb was now exposed, bereft of its insect cloak—the ivory-white skeleton of a man.

22

Nina fell mute as she backpedaled. Her heel caught in a tangle of thick grass, and she spilled backward, then scrambled in a hasty crab walk to put as much distance as possible between herself and the awful sight. Chills racked her body. Every hair on her body rose with goose flesh.

Twisting over on her hands and knees, Nina clambered to her feet and sprinted blindly, quickly smacking into someone who knocked her to the ground.

Her throat was now raw from screaming. She'd already earned several cuts and scrapes from where she'd fallen, and knew that if she survived until tomorrow, a couple of well-earned bruises were sure to blossom in ugly blues and purples, especially on her knees and elbows.

Nina cowered and raised her arms in defense. "Please don't hurt me!"

The buzzing ceased, and the normalcy of nature slowly returned to the field. The air was hot and close. Animals bleated their usual tunes, and Nina became simply a woman in an orchard clearing. Her eyes were squeezed shut, and she'd clung to fistfuls of grass and dirt from her seat on the ground. When he spoke, she flinched and held tighter to the earth, as if it would help her world stop spinning.

"So you know, this isn't how I wanted you to find out." Born of wistful daydreams and afternoon dozes, his voice was soporific and smooth.

Nina peeked at Colin, the sun shining from behind him as it had on the day she first encountered him. The effect was one of an angelic aura, emphasizing his lean muscles beneath his formfitting jeans and buttoned-down shirt. For the first time, she realized the outfit had always been the same. Not even the shirt changed from its crisp cream color. He was a man frozen in time, at the peak of his prime.

Nina studied his features. The aquiline shape of his nose wasn't as severe as Greta's, yet it was surely a feature inherited from his mother. His jaw was stronger than Greta's, his lips full rather than thin, inviting, and alluring. How could this man have killed his father and tormented his mother for decades? How could he not . . . be alive?

Colin held out his hand to her. She gawked at it like it was an accosting spider.

"Please don't look at me like that," he said. "You have to understand, this is the first time I've gotten to live some of the life that was taken from me. I never wanted to hurt you, Nina."

Despite the man's beauty, and the intimacy they'd shared, it couldn't undo what she now knew. "I believe you," Nina said, with a coldness in her voice that was liable to break both their hearts. She got to her feet on her own, taking no joy in the disappointment on his face when he dropped his hand back to his side. "I am hurt, though. But it's not about how you hurt me—how could you do this to your mother? She loves you. She's been asking for your forgiveness for decades, and you've given her nothing."

He moved toward what was left of his physical form and gestured at the skeleton with the flick of a hand. "And what about what she did to me?"

"What *she* did to *you*?"

Portentous, slate-gray clouds loomed overhead, reflected in Colin's stormy eyes. Though he held a physical form, Nina perceived a slightness to him— an out-of-focus quality to his face, a transparence to his body. When she looked directly at any of his features, it was gone. Yet in the periphery of her vision, the effect persisted. Colin was diminished since she'd last seen him, and it wasn't just from the shadows thrown from above. It was something else, and if it was for the reason she thought, he and Greta didn't have much time.

"She was supposed to protect me." He beat his fist against his chest when he said 'me.' "She was my mother. She was supposed to protect me from him. Not stay, not let him kill me." Colin fell to his knees and wrapped his arms around Nina's waist, pressing the side of his face to her stomach. "You—you're a true mother. You got away from 'your Henry' and are doing everything you can to protect Holden."

Nina gritted her teeth, and the roar of a storm welled within her, breaking through a dam that had long been weakening. She shoved him away. "You have no idea what it's like to be a mother. There is no rulebook—there is no right or wrong. I don't know that what I'm doing is the right thing any more than your mother did. She couldn't have known what was going to happen back then. Leaving might've gone the same way. You can't hold on to what-if's and should'ves. You think you're haunting Greta—it's Henry who's got the last laugh. He's still poisoning you both."

Dense clouds knit in the sky, urged by a southerly wind. Raindrops flecked Nina's skin, bringing a shiver across her arms. She watched as each drop left a translucent sheen on Colin, like it was erasing him slowly, washing him away.

Nina searched her memory. "I've never seen you on a rainy day. The sun sustains you in this form somehow, doesn't it?"

He nodded and drew closer to her. The touch of his fingers on her shoulder was like the last of the warm air brushing against her skin. "I have to go. What did you mean when you said it's poisoning us both? Is Greta okay?"

She reached up to caress his cheek. It was like stroking a cloud. "I don't know for certain, but each time we find more bees dead, she seems to get weaker. I thought it might just be from a broken heart." She crossed her arms and shook her head. "Now, I think you are somehow bound together, keeping each other tied to the orchard."

Colin looked up to the sky, a faint wisp of himself. When he turned his attention to her, his irises were two silver discs against the darkening sky. Water dripped down his cheeks, and she wasn't sure which were from the rain or from his tears. "I just wanted a chance, you know? Until you came, I was caught in a spiral from which I'd never thought I'd be free. Then I met you, Nina. I wish we could've explored a life together."

The rain hastened, coming down in heavy teardrops. Her hair hung in wet rivulets and her dress clung to her body. Every fiber of her being longed to tell him she felt the same way. Instead, Nina stepped close and planted a soft kiss on the ghost of his lips. He tasted like sunshine and honey. Nina drew back and let out tears of her own to mingle with the rain.

"Seems to me, Colin," she said, "that even if it wasn't the life you imagined for yourself, the orchard has given you a chance. Holding onto grudges and regrets only keeps you tied down to a past you can't change. There'll always be things we wish were different. Things that happened that weren't our fault, things that happened that were. What matters is what you choose to do with the time you have left."

With her final words, the last fragments of Colin floated away on strengthening winds. Nina stood weighted to the spot and sobbed into her hands, rain pelting her from above.

After a few minutes, Nina wiped her face, brushed back her hair, and ran back to the farmhouse, the torrents of the coming storm hot on her heels.

23

The front door slammed shut behind Nina and echoed through the foyer.

"Greta?" Lightning cracked outside, followed by thunder. Nina wrung out her hair over the entryway rug and shook off what excess water she could. "Greta!"

The old woman's slender figure descended the stairs and held a firm finger to her lips. "Quiet, child. I've only just gotten Holden to settle down. Though I fear this storm won't keep it that way."

Brilliant light flashed through the foyer windows, illuminating the furniture and their shadows at odd, sharp angles. The electricity flickered, then went out. Greta rushed down the last of the steps and briefly embraced Nina. "You're soaked. Come, let's get you dry. I'll make you a cup of hot tea, and we can light some candles."

Nina huddled over her tea, letting the steam rise and warm her face. Greta threw a shawl over her shoulders and rubbed up and down her arms before sitting next to her at the kitchen island. The storm rattled the windows. Nina kept an ear out for Holden but hadn't heard him wake yet.

"We must be in the thick of it now," Greta said, as she fixed up her own cup of tea. "Sounds like it's traveling fast, though."

Nina mumbled her agreement about the nature of the storm. She gazed down into her teacup, unsure of what to say to Greta.

"Do you want some apple pie?" Greta asked. Making a pie together from the apples from the oldest trees had become a weekly routine of theirs. Half of this week's pie remained, sitting on the counter, covered with tinfoil.

Nina shook her head.

"You sure? I think the oven will still work. I could heat it up, give you a scoop of vanilla ice cream on the side?" Greta was going to great lengths to comfort her. Nina realized she was uncomfortable too.

"Sure." Nina shrugged. She watched as Greta went about preparing the pie. Being able to move about with some purpose, any purpose, seemed to calm the woman. Nina rallied around her tea and warmed her hands on the cup. "So . . ."

Greta shut the oven door and stood straight. "So."

"I don't know how to do this, Greta." Nina helped herself to an extra spoonful of honey, then paused as she lifted the cup to her mouth. Did Colin control the bees that made this honey? Was he . . . possessing them? She had so many questions left unspoken, with no answers on the horizon.

Greta faced the backyard as lightning zigzagged across the sky. She turned about and leaned the small of her back against the sink to face Nina. "Child, none of us know how. I'm sorry you got caught in the middle of all this. Clearly, you and Colin have spent some time together, right?"

Nina nodded. She dabbed a tissue at her runny nose.

"Much as I'd like to know every detail, I would never ask you to betray his confidence like that. I just want him to be happy, at peace." Greta wiped her hands across her eyes and sniffled.

"He showed me nothing but tenderness and care. But peace? That's something he's going to have to choose for himself." Nina ran her finger along the rim of her cup. "This is all so . . . unbelievable. I mean, I touched him. Really touched him, like he was alive. I don't understand how that can be."

Greta came back over and rested against the island countertop. After a few minutes of silence, listening to the clap and boom of the storm, Greta fixed her eyes on the honey bear jar. She picked it up and held it high, scrutinizing it as if it could whisper secrets to her.

"No." Greta shook her head. "It's not possible."

Nina stood and joined Greta in looking at the bottle. "What?"

"Do you remember when you first ate the honey? I know you refused for some time after the incident when I gave Holden some in the general store, without your permission."

Nina's legs wobbled. Lightheadedness overtook her. She touched her fingers to her lips. "You made a thermos of tea for me. I remember being so angry that you put honey in it. That was the first day I saw him. And before that, I swear, in the orchard, Holden was looking at someone I couldn't see."

Greta rested a hand over her own heart and the vial. "The honey allows us to see him. My gran used to say that bees are a conduit between the living and the dead. The honey *did* taste differently after he passed." Nina let out an anguished wail and collapsed into her hands. Her shoulders shook with soft sobs. Greta rubbed her back in small, soothing circles. "You love him, don't you?"

Nina looked up at Greta with red-rimmed eyes, pleading for answers from the old woman. "I do. I can't help it, I do." Nina held Greta's hands and rested her forehead against Greta's. "What are we gonna do? I can't stay here, not after the sheriff came looking for me. It's not safe for either of us. But it would break my heart to leave you. Both of you."

Greta pursed her lips, seemingly in an effort to hold back more tears. She stroked Nina's hair and wrapped an arm around her. "Me too, child. Though if you stay, I'm not sure how much time we've got left anyhow. Why don't we get some rest and see how things look in the light of day tomorrow—"

High-pitched cries cut through the noise of the storm. Nina's stomach churned, her anxiety like a shot of espresso straight to her nervous system. Holden needed tending to.

"I don't think I could sleep right now if I tried. I'm afraid of the dreams I'd have. After I settle down Holden, I think I'll come back down for another cup of tea, if you want to join me."

Greta bestowed Nina with a solemn nod as Nina exited the kitchen. Before she could hurry up the stairs, she stopped in the foyer. The front door was ajar. Strobes of lightning flickered nightmarishly through the inch-wide opening. As she shut it, she surmised that the winds must've really strengthened to force such a sturdy door open.

When she turned around, a splash of yellow on

the entryway table caught her attention. The blood drained from her face as she drew near. She ran her fingertips over their soft, bruised petals.

Daffodils.

Holden's cries had a frightened undertone to them that worried Nina. She climbed the stairs two at a time. By now, she could pinpoint what his different noises meant. She could tell from across the house whether his grunts were an effort to poop or get at a shiny object, whether his cries were whining for momma or indicative of pain. Panic surged through her veins. All she could focus on was getting to him as fast as she could.

Nina sprinted down the hall and skidded to a stop in front of the open guest room door.

Open.

In the dark-shrouded room, Nina saw the silhouette of a man hovering over Holden's crib, arms reaching in to pick up her son. His movements were slow and calculated, like he knew she was watching. His back was broad, his arms corded with proudly gym-built muscles. There was no roughness in his movements as he moved to pick up Holden and hug him into his chest, absorbing the child into his inky shadow. He gently rocked and shushed Holden until the cries ceased, then held the boy out at arm's length and tossed him high into the air.

24

Nina thought the world was going to open up and swallow her in that moment. She rushed forward, knowing she was too far away to catch him. "John—"

John flashed a smile, teeth almost like fangs in the dark, and caught Holden easily. The child squealed with delight and giggled at his father.

Her entire body shook with anger and terror. She considered trying to snatch Holden away from him and run. But where to? She didn't know if she could get the truck keys in time. Holden was likely to get hurt in the process. And what about Greta?

No, she knew exactly what she had to do. Nina took a shuddering breath and ran her hands along her body, as if she could wipe her fear away. Brushing her hair behind her ear, she leaned against the door frame. "You always did know how to make him laugh."

John propped Holden on his hip and approached her. He cupped her cheek gently. She almost believed the relief and warmth in his eyes were genuine. "Did you see the daffodils?"

She nodded, leaning into his touch. "You didn't have to do that."

He pulled her close. "Yes, I did." He caressed her brow lightly with his knuckles. "I'm sorry, Nina. You just make me so crazy, sometimes I lose control of myself."

Nina closed her eyes, letting tears fall. "It's . . . okay now." Her breath hitched as she inhaled. "How did you find me?"

John eased back from her, his face pained. "Didn't you want to be found? Isn't that why you called your mother?"

Holden wiggled in John's grip. He tickled Holden, who scrunched up his face cutely and giggled. Nina stared at them both. Every smile from her baby killed her. She couldn't share the horror she felt.

She crossed her arms and dug her fingernails into her skin, cursing herself for that moment of weakness. "Yes, yes, of course."

"Good." John pecked her on the cheek. It was all she could do not to cringe. "Let's go downstairs. I'm starving." He led them down the hall to the landing.

As she followed him, she felt like she was walking in her own funeral procession. How could she have been so careless? As soon as she saw that sheriff sniffing around, she should've packed up and left immediately. Staying here, allowing herself a small measure of happiness—she let her guard down. Nina had actually thought she was on the path to being a good mother, a protector. Failure had grabbed her by the ankles and ripped her feet right out from under her. The lights flickered as they reached the foyer.

John paused on the threadbare country rug.

Lightning flashed and distorted his face. "Please, honey, would you point me in the direction of our host?"

Nina stopped. "Why? What're you going to do to her?"

The smack across her face rang out, and blinding pain followed. Holden was struck dumb for only a second, then screamed at the top of his lungs. Bent over, cradling her cheek that reverberated with the force of his hit, Nina sensed John standing over her.

"I don't know why you insist on questioning me. I love you so damn much, and look at what you made me do. Now where is she?"

Nina pointed weakly to the kitchen door. It was perhaps one of her most shameful acts. Yet, Holden's cries wrenched her, and she wasn't so much worried about what John would do to her as what would happen to Holden if she blacked out. She hoped Greta would understand. Maybe even Greta had heard the altercation and had time to get away.

"John, she's in her eighties. You can't think—" Nina's voice was barely above a whisper.

Rain pelted the windows. John raised his hand higher in the air and delivered another blow across her cheekbone, hitting her ear. Nina collapsed to one knee, the side of her face stinging, ablaze.

John reached down to help her to her feet. His hand hovered over where he'd hit her. He eyed her with concern. "Nina, be careful. I could really hurt you."

She did her best to act as if nothing had happened and held her arms out toward Holden. "Please, let me hold him," she stammered. "I can calm him down."

John stared at her, his eyes going dead. "I can calm him down just as well as you, you know." He handed over Holden to her, and tears welled in her eyes. "But to show you how much I truly love you, I'll allow you this."

Nina squeezed Holden against her chest. John jutted his chin at the kitchen door. "You first, my love."

25

Nina teased open the swinging door, the usual creak drowned out against the stilted rain. She entered slowly, holding her hand over her baby's head to shield him. Like a rabbit caught in headlights, Nina froze at the sight of Greta, still as stone and crouched behind the door with the eye of the rifle pointed at Nina's face.

Carrying on and pretending as best she could that she hadn't seen a thing, Nina continued toward the kitchen island, obeying the quick nod from Greta to move out of the way. Nina desperately wanted to shake her head no, that as much as she hated John, she couldn't bear to have him die in front of Holden. But doing so might well cost Greta her life in return.

John's arm lashed out to keep the door from swinging shut on him. Nina stiffened, and her eyes involuntarily darted, giving away Greta's position; John forced the door back against its hinges to slam into Greta; the old woman pulled the rifle's trigger.

The gun went off, a flare and a thunder to rival that of the storm. Nina's ears rang as she dove behind the counter. She clamped her hands over Holden's ears, though some damage was probably already done. The boy's mouth opened wide with screams she couldn't hear. She stroked her son with one hand as she inched forward on her elbows to the corner of the island.

Bile burned the back of her throat as the endless horrific possibilities of what lay beyond flashed across her eyelids. Nina braced Holden as safely as she could behind the countertop and allowed barely a sliver of her eye to peek around the corner.

She saw nothing of the expected rivers of blood across the floor. Instead, John stumbled, back to her, as he wrestled with Greta for the gun, the stock and barrel jolting violently as they tussled. Nina swung around and planted her back flush against the wood paneling, still clutching Holden. His tiny hands clung to her shoulders with such ferocity that she thought she might lose what little composure she had left. Her mind in overdrive, she bit her lip to stifle a cry.

Unless Greta could get a lucky shot off, this was a battle she was unlikely to win, despite the old woman's many surprising capabilities. Nina's hearing came back in fits and starts. The storm was abating. Past the two figures locked in combat, she hastily considered an escape route.

The swinging door wasn't an option. There was no way she could sneak safely by with Holden, past the grappling. Her eyes traveled over the sink, the counters. The briefest irrational notion called to her —grab a knife from the butcher's block and join the fray. She imagined herself brandishing it bravely to —do what? *Kill* him?

Nina shook her head. That would mean setting Holden down, and she couldn't guarantee he wouldn't wander over. She would die before letting anything happen to him.

Above the sink, a calm glow filtered through the bay window. The sun was rising. She and Greta must've stayed up later than she'd realized.

Nina looked to her right, the back door ten feet away. She didn't have much choice; she was going to have to risk going out the back. Squatting, bracing Holden over her shoulder, she was a coiled spring, ready to unleash.

Mentally, Nina counted to three, then burst forth from behind the island and dashed for the door. Just as quickly, she skittered to stop as John leaped out in front of her, the rifle pointed square at her chest. If John were to shoot her now, she and Holden would both surely die.

"Are you really leaving me again, at a time like this? Have you no heart, woman?"

The storm had fully ceased, sunlight struggling through its remaining clouds. The kitchen grew eerily silent. Nina edged to the side so the rifle wasn't aimed at Holden. She couldn't hear anything from Greta, and didn't dare turn and look, unwilling to risk John's ire.

Her own body had crossed a line, something far beyond fear, anger, exhaustion—a strange stillness that said *I have nothing left to give.*

"I was trying to get Holden out of harm's way." The tremor in her voice was gone. She sounded far away from herself, as if the lips speaking those words were from someone else, detached.

John rammed the rifle into her cheek, cutting

the skin near her teeth until the trickle of blood ran metallic against her tongue. He pressed the end of the barrel deeper into her bruising skin, hot metal against flesh, appearing to wait for some reaction he wanted to elicit from her. She gave nothing. Yet an internal, wicked grin curled within. Somewhere in the back of her mind, she wondered if part of her had finally broken beyond repair.

"That's all you've got to say for yourself?" He snorted at her. "Not even an ounce of worry for old Johnny, huh? You always did love that little runt more than me."

Again, she gave him nothing. Then she expelled a giant wad of bloody spittle onto the floor. In a trance, she watched it spread on the tile like a red rose in bloom. It might well have been an emblem of their marriage.

She cocked her head to face him, letting the barrel of the rifle drag from cheek to forehead, and locked defiant eyes with his. The seconds ticked by on the hands of the bird clock above the sink basin, echoing softly in the farmhouse kitchen. A blue jay chimed the top of the hour. John jumped—the trance was broken.

To her mild surprise, he lowered the rifle. He stalked around her in a couple circles like an angry vulture before wandering back toward the swinging door. In a careful turn, Nina spied Greta, limp on the floor. She rushed past John to kneel and press a hand to her neck. Greta's pulse thumped weakly against Nina's fingers.

John grabbed Nina by the back of her collar and tossed her away from the old woman. Nina cush-ioned Holden as she recovered and stared at John, all her rage flowing through her now, present in her expression. No, John was not like a vulture. He was a dog. Looking him in the eyes had always been something he perceived as a challenge. This was just the first time she'd had the backbone to do it.

Instead of yelling at her again, he took her chin in his calloused hand with the softest touch. John's eyes were dull brown things, filled with the simple anger of a simple man. They seemed to widen in surprise.

"You've changed," he said.

The words stung like an accusation. Had she? She wanted to run her hands along her body to check, to lay her hand over her heart as if she could feel any real difference from the woman who'd stolen away in the middle of the night months ago.

John released her chin roughly, propped up the rifle next to him, and slid into one of the chairs at the island. He slapped his hands flat on the counter. "I'm hungry."

Holden squirmed in her arms. Nina worried about the damage the gunshot had done to his hearing. But all she could do at this moment was settle him into the high chair and promise to feed him as well. Nina fetched a glass of water from the sink and slid it over to John, who gulped it thirstily.

"What would you like to eat, honey?" The endearment came out bland as dry toast.

John's gaze fell on the leftover apple pie sitting in the center of the kitchen island. As his hands plucked up the thin tinfoil, she wanted to lurch across and snatch it away from him. He wasn't deserving. Something in her posture must've shown this, because his eyes narrowed. "Is that apple pie?"

He lifted the glass dish and sniffed. "Smells delicious."

She swallowed her irritation, brushed her hair hastily from her face. "It sure is. Made it from scratch myself."

"Did you?" John smiled. "I'm impressed. I would *love* to try a piece of your pie, Nina."

26

Nina pulled the reheated pie out of the oven, the homey apple scent filling the air. She'd given Holden some cereal to tide him over. After setting the pie down on the counter, she retrieved a knife from the butcher's block. Up until then, she'd gone through the motions, her domestic tasks in service to John a well-trodden path that was terrifyingly easy to re-adopt.

Her skin crawled under John's watchful gaze, and she paused before plunging the knife into the piecrust. After using it to transport a slice onto the plate next to the vanilla bean ice cream she'd already scooped, Nina walked to the sink and held the knife up like a mirror. In the wide blade, she saw her own face, dirty and drawn and disappointed. A wildness glinted in her eyes that spoke to what she should do, what Greta would want her to do. Did she have it in her?

She half-turned and, in her hesitation, John was upon her. He grabbed her wrist and angled the knife down, the cold spear of metal sinking into her gut. Nina moaned, gripping the handle, and slid to the floor. Her mouth opened and closed like a fish on dry land. Bitter tears streamed down her cheeks.

John stood over her, grabbing the warm slice of pie with melting ice cream and taking a bite off his fork with a flourish. "Thanks for the pie."

He sat next to Holden's high chair and devoured the family treat while blood poured from Nina's gut. She did her best to curb her instinct to pull out the knife. If she did, she would surely bleed out.

John's smacking and swallowing was grotesque in the stifling quiet of the kitchen. It reminded her of a dog lapping up its dinner gleefully, the slap of the tongue on the roof of the mouth, the dreadful gulps without even tasting the dessert. Nina tried several times to find her voice.

"I wasn't going to stab you, John."

"Why ever not?" he said matter-of-factly. His eyes narrowed at her. "You clearly don't know how to love me properly. Can't even care enough to hate me properly, either?"

She thought she knew the depths of his cruelty, but clearly it knew no bounds. "You want to know why?" She coughed and was alarmed when her hand came away with pinkish red froth from her lips. "Because despite all you've done, despite how you've tried to push me, I'm not like you. I won't become the person who killed my son's father."

His fork grated and scraped against the plate as he continued to eat. He paused to point the prongs at her. "Pity. Your righteousness will cost you your life and your son. Was it worth it?"

Nina gazed past him at Greta's limp shoes, lying disturbingly horizontal on the floor. She considered his words. Their truth entered her like poison. She'd failed Holden one final time. Her son held his arms out to her, ready to get out of the high chair, his cherubic little face confused as to why she wasn't coming. His lip was drooping—he was going to cry any second now. Then came the wail, a dim reflection of the ache within herself. He was doomed to be raised by John, to become his father. Nina held fast to the last fragments of her life, love as much as hatred helping her cling on.

Did Greta wish she'd put an end to Henry earlier? She thought of Colin and his resentment toward his mother. When Holden grew into a young man, would his memories of Nina be colored with the same ire? John would make certain it was so, and it was more than she could bear. Nina had known John would never let her get away. Should she have poisoned his dinner or fed him extra sleeping pills? She shook her head, bordering on a tick, death throes nipping at her heels.

There were no answers. As she stared at John, a cold sweat breaking across her forehead, something flicked against the bay window above the sink.

Then another.

And another.

Both looked to see miniscule black bodies pounding themselves against the panes, so numerous they almost sounded like the rain from earlier.

On the other side of the room, there was a groan. Greta was stirring at the sound—Nina could see her feet moving.

Emotions, the last Nina had left, welled up inside her. Nina began to speak.

She began to sing to the bees.

Oh, what small mercy can this be?
Has my love searched his heart and come to aid me?

Gone, I am not, and so the bees I will tell
John, my husband, your place belongs in hell
Ripe with life and love, apples are birthed from the
trees
Mother and son are one; our home lies with the bees
For what's true is love and thy heart, still
And I hope we'll live happily forever after at Orchard
Hill

Though each note delivered fresh lacerations from the knife wound, Nina sang with striking clarity and volume. Her voice was beautiful and haunting, melodic and magnificent. The swarm at the window mirrored her song in miraculous swoops and swirls, patterned on the glass.

John bounced his knee, agitated. He shoved the last forkful of pie into his overfull cheeks then started yelling at them all to shut up.

The pie caught in his throat. He wrapped his hands around his neck. The color drained from his face, a hint of purple creeping into his complexion, the fruit of the orchard's eldest trees now blocking his air.

John emitted muted, pathetic noises as he choked. His veins bulged up and down his temples and neck. Nina couldn't help him even if she wanted to, not with a kitchen knife sticking out of her gut like some crude macho flag, not with her world dimming around her, worn at the edges but framing John clearly before her.

A desperate sheen of sweat broke out on John's heavy brow, and he began throwing himself against the edge of the counter, over and over and over. It wasn't until a sizeable chunk of half-chewed apple flew out of his mouth and landed on the floor with a *plop* that she grasped that he'd been giving himself the Heimlich. Doubling over in harsh fits of coughing, his hands on his knees and revolting trails of spittle glomming onto the tile, the normal color returned to his face. He rose, arms back, then inhaled and exhaled in great exaggerated fashion, running his meaty hands along the sides of his body where his lungs were.

The regurgitated piece of apple lay by Nina's haphazard, almost useless legs. She cringed as it twitched, and a maggot forced its way out and wriggled onto the floor. Nina looked up to see John turning green as he scrutinized what was left on his plate. Again, he doubled over, this time with melodramatic vomiting, forcing a finger down his throat to bring up the rest of the pie in a wet, goopy lump on the floor. More maggots squirmed out of it.

The man stared entranced at the pile, then craned his neck to glare at Nina. He swiped the plate off the island, his fork scattering to the floor with a clang, and shoved it in her face. Nina scooted her heels back and turned her face away from the foul stench that came from both the plate and John's breath.

"*You* did this!" John lifted the dessert plate and smashed it on the floor, the ceramic scattering in a million tiny shards. Dimly, Nina realized Holden had thought John was playing around when he was choking, but now his giggles turned to terrified screams.

John reached around the corner, grabbed the rifle, and cocked it dramatically. He aimed it at Nina's head. At the moment he fired, movement blurred between the bullet and Nina. Nina screamed, flaring the pain of the blade in her side. She again clutched to hold the knife still. However, it was difficult not to move with the racking sobs that came flooding out when she saw what had intercepted the bullet intended for her.

John had shot Greta.

On the floor between them, Greta lay on her back, nursing a gunshot wound in her hip. Nina scooted close to the woman and cradled her head as best she could. "No, no, no . . ." Nina repeated like a chant.

Greta lifted a slender finger, sticky with blood,

and shushed her. Greta moved her mouth, but Nina couldn't hear a word she said. Nina squirmed down as far as she could, without getting the knife deeper into her own side, and put her ear near the woman's mouth. Greta's breath was a hot whisper against her skin.

"Quiet, my child, it's going to be okay," Greta said. "You're going to make it through this. When you do, make sure you pay a visit to my lawyer, Mr. Quimby, in town. He'll make sure you and that precious boy are well taken care of."

Greta stroked Nina's hair. Tears dripped down Nina's cheeks.

"Nina." Greta coughed and was quiet, her last words barely audible. "Take care of your sweet son and don't . . . tell the bees I'm gone . . ."

The tension went out of Greta's body. Her wrinkles smoothed, and she looked strikingly like she did in the picture of her on the day Colin was born. Hyperventilating a little, Nina laid her gently on the floor. Waves of nausea rolled over her. Her hands and feet were cold and numb. Nina had done her best to maintain her strength, but she wasn't going to be able to fend off death much longer.

Pressing her forearm on the counter, she lifted herself unsteadily to her feet, screaming in agony all the while. John stood, rifle hanging limply at his side, unable to tear his eyes from Greta's dead body.

"Yes," Nina hissed at him. "Look at what you've done."

Hand over hand, Nina limped with great effort toward the back door, blood trickling behind her. The sweet scent of honey rode on the air. Along the windows, the bees followed her, banging against the glass, cracking it in spidery bursts.

Nina rested her hand on the brass knob and glared at John. "You know, perhaps you're right after all." Nina cast a glance at Greta, her silver-streaked hair spread out around her. "As a great woman once said to me, a mother sometimes has to do things that make her uncomfortable to protect her child."

Twisting the knob, Nina stepped aside as the door roared open, the swarm of bees bursting forth, aiming for John. Their hurricane hum enveloped the screaming man as he cowered, puny in their presence. She could no longer tell man from insect in the dark, churning cloud.

One by one, bees dropped lifelessly to the floor, reminding her of the time Holden spilled crafting pom-poms. Yet instead of feeling frustrated and slightly amused, she was left feeling forlorn, looking at all their black-and-yellow bodies. John swatted and fought, flailing backward against the oven, every inch of him covered in welts from the stings. Nina moved weakly toward them.

The buzzing quieted as the black swarm littered the floor. Nina's heart, already broken open by the early morning events, fractured even further at the realization that Colin had spent the last of the bees to save her, to avenge his mother.

Colin was gone. Greta was gone.

John was gone.

Alone, Nina hobbled over and collapsed against the legs of the high chair. She sang softly to calm Holden. She wanted to go to the foyer and try to ring for help, but her legs were two useless logs. Her skin tingled, her consciousness waned, and she sang to her son until she could no longer fight back the weight of her eyelids and so drifted away.

28

Someone jostled Nina about, knocking her flat on the cold kitchen tile, lifting at her calves and shoulders. She felt like she was floating . . . until she was strapped down onto what she began to realize was a stretcher. There was much coordinated shouting around her. She fought hard to pry open her eyes and peered up into the white mustached face of someone familiar that she couldn't quite place. He leaned down close to her, old coffee on his breath, his eyes kind and words soothing—that's what was off about the sheriff. She'd expected the same malice in him she'd seen in John.

His gruff voice assured her, "Nina, we're going to get you to the hospital. We've got your son—he's okay."

Paramedics lifted the stretcher, and the sheriff held open the swinging kitchen door to carry her through. Nina tried to sit up, to look for Greta, to search for Colin, but the paramedics urged her to lie back down.

Nina only caught a glimpse of more EMTs by the oven. Before the kitchen door swung closed, she heard them talking.

"This is just like the Henry Richardson case they tell spooky stories about at the station."

"Yeah, but this guy's not all stung up. The lucky bastard is still breathing."

The door closed and Nina was being carted through the foyer and out the front door. She pressed her hand to her chest, her heart thumping wildly, her breath coming raggedly. The knife stung her, and she howled in pain.

The paramedic at her head yelled, "She's going into shock. Hurry—!"

Black spots littered Nina's vision of the bright blue sky overhead, drawing her toward darkness.

29

Nina stood at the foot of Greta's fresh grave, surrounded by the four gnarled apple trees now as familiar to her as old friends. Their presence comforted her in her sorrow. A cool wind whispered through the leaves and caught the hem of Nina's pastel-yellow dress, making it dance in the breeze. She gripped the stems of a dozen yellow roses clustered together by a black-and-white striped ribbon. She let the thorns dig into her palms before setting them on Greta's headstone. Nina had enlisted the funeral home to add to the original inscription, which now read, *'Here lies Greta Richardson. Mother of honey and bees, Forever remembered among the apple trees.'*

She hoped Greta would like it. Nina hiked up her dress and kneeled beside the grave. "I can't believe you left Orchard Hill to me. I don't know if I deserve it, and I'll never be able to repay you for what you've done for me and my son." She got to her feet, pushed her shoulders back, and gazed out at the expanse of the orchard. Her fingers wrapped around the vial containing the queen bee that hung from the necklace she wore—Greta's necklace. "But

I'll do everything I can to keep Orchard Hill alive, and to make you proud."

Nina wiped away a tear and made her way back to the house. She wished for nothing more than to be coming back to have tea with Greta on the wrap-around porch. The pollen-yellow house at the crest of the hill sat like an empty beehive awaiting a new colony to form, to bring it back to buzzing life. Whether Nina was up to the task remained to be seen, and, despite her brave face, she yearned for Greta's straight talk and the way she called her 'child.'

When she reached the bottom of the porch steps, the black-lacquered front door creaked open and John walked through, carrying Holden. Each time she saw his face, her stomach flopped. Greta had willed the far-reaching acreage of Orchard Hill and the farmhouse to Nina, and it'd only been a couple weeks since they'd buried Greta on the orchard property. She thought that's what Greta would've wanted.

Nina held her side as she carefully made her way up the steps. Last thing she wanted to do was pop a stitch. She joined John at the porch railing, looking out over the rolling hills of apple trees in the late season. The air was sweet and rich with their decay.

John hadn't said much of anything since that night. He seemed to be struggling. Murdering someone will do that to you. Despite clear evidence that John had killed Greta, somehow Sheriff Wesson had chalked it up to a bizarre accident in self-defense—a man going in search of his wife, a woman defending her property, a tragic accident born of confusion and high emotions. A complicated domestic squabble better brushed under the rug than dragged out in a court of law. Upsetting though it was, it didn't surprise her.

The sheriff had made it very clear to Nina the downsides, to her and her child, of pursuing legal action against John, a cop. Especially in such a small town.

'Think of what that would do to Orchard Hill. How badly would that tarnish what you've inherited from Greta Richardson?' he'd asked her. There had been a curious fear in his voice. Nina suspected that what really frightened the mighty sheriff were the bees of Orchard Hill. She'd delivered a wan smile and acquiesced.

Nina wasn't sure when John was going to break out of his stupor, or when the other shoe was going to drop on their idyllic orchard life. She gripped the railing and watched him, wondering what he was thinking. The sense of a storm brewing beneath the surface of his placid exterior unnerved her.

The sun shifted in the sky, illuminating him from behind. Nina blinked, then blinked again. John's hair was a dark, muddy black. By some trick of the light, the sun bestowed a golden halo around his head. Nina stiffened, but it passed so quickly she couldn't be sure what she'd seen.

The day passed by, languid and serene as had the days in the weeks before. John didn't say more than a handful of words to her. When he did, his energy still seemed focused on some internal battle within. Today, however, Nina attempted to observe him with fresh eyes. Pensive, she tried to keep the puzzle from showing on her face in the long stretches of silence between them.

That evening, after John was well asleep and

Holden was tucked into his crib, Nina awoke. Though they were in a different house and a different bed, she couldn't help but feel a sense of déjà vu from that night she'd run away.

She searched John's slumbering face, watching a mixture of tense emotions come over him as he slept fitfully. The lines in his forehead deepened, and he frowned, his eyes darting back and forth beneath his eyelids. She raised a tentative hand and stroked the side of his face. When he didn't wake, she slipped out of bed, pulling on one of Greta's silky black robes, and crept down to the kitchen.

Stealing out the back door, she took a match and lit a red candle that she'd found among Greta's possessions. She'd been reading up further on how to properly tend to the bees, despite not having spotted one since that day. Still, she had a promise to keep to Greta. Walking amongst the silent beehives, small, white, boxy mausoleums in the dark, she covered each one in black cloth.

After she was done, Nina cradled the scarlet candle in her hands, roamed amongst the dormant hives, and sang to the bees once more. She sang to them of her own life and what had led her to this point. She sang of her joys and regrets, her happinesses and her sorrows, of her love for Holden, of her love for Orchard Hill.

Her sonorous melody took on a sepulchral tone. The jade leaves of the apple trees shuddered, restless with her words. And then Nina sang, not of Greta's death, but of *John's*. She told the bees of the death of her son's father.

As she concluded her song, a booming, furious voice thundered behind her in the night air. Nina did her best to calm her nerves as she spun around.

"Just what do you think you're doing—"

John stalked toward her, moving in a jerky, stiff-legged fashion like his body couldn't make up its mind whether to throttle her or run away. His face contorted in a grimace of agony.

Nina inhaled through her nose and exhaled slowly through her mouth. She trusted in Greta and the bees. The vial nestled in her bosom levitated, and the image of John through the glass offered a comical funhouse mirror view of the man, blunting her fear of the monstrous promise in his eyes.

She clasped the phial delicately and held the crimson candle up to it. The queen bee had returned to life. Nina uncorked the stopper from the top. The bee unfurled its wings, ruby stained-glass windows in the light, and rose high into the air.

Soon, a spectral legion of bees joined her, a brand-new colony, born of old. They gathered and coalesced in the sky, visible against the moon. Nina swore their outline was reminiscent of the four ancestral apple trees, set upon safeguarding those tied to the land of the orchard.

John had almost reached her, his outstretched hands strained inches from her face. The swarm descended, sharp as a blade's edge, and flew directly into John's heart. They passed through him and, as the bees vacated his physical form, the mass carried John's translucent, wretched spirit away with them, deep into the night.

Nina rushed over to John's body and lifted him in her arms. Her hand trembled as she reached out to cup his cheek, hoping, yet never letting herself believe it could be true. His golden hair was like phoenix fire in the red candlelight, his cheeks soft, his lips full.

When his eyes opened at last, they penetrated her with their silver-gray radiance. He stood with grace and held her against his chest.

Nina's lips parted. "Colin—"

He lifted her chin gently and silenced her with a kiss. Their mouths welded together, the sweet taste of honey on their tongues. His strong hands embraced the small of her back as he pulled her flush against his body, firm and lean, not overly muscled and thick like John. As they kissed, every part of Nina hummed with excitement. From the top of her head to the tips of her toes, she was filled with bliss and contentment. For the first time, she truly felt like she was home.

30

S ummer retreated and gave way to fall's colorful
windswept leaves. Winter snow-drifted by, a
season of fireside snuggles and hot chocolate. They
watched spring stroll in, and once the ground dried
from the rain showers and summer heat again returned to Orchard Hill, Nina, Colin, and Holden
ventured into the orchard for a picnic.

"Do you want to go to the wildflower field?" Nina
asked, as she and Colin lightly swayed their clasped
hands.

Colin shook his head, then smirked. "No, I think
I've spent enough time there."

She laughed. "Okay, then where?"

"Let's go to the ancestral trees. I, uh . . . think it
would be nice."

Nina nodded. She wouldn't mind visiting Greta's
grave as well, but she was also fine if he wanted to
leave that unsaid. Their time together hadn't been
some fairytale *happily ever after*. Colin could be
naive at times. He tended to hog the hot water, eat
honey by the bucketful, and leave cupboards open
like he was a poltergeist. He'd smiled at this compar-
ison, which made her happy, though they never

spoke much about his time as a ghost. Had he been a ghost? Or had he possessed the bees? She'd wrestled with these questions, not voicing many of them to Colin because, on the tip of her tongue, they turned crass and unimportant.

The only thing he'd shared about his experience was his incredible loneliness and inability to let go of his resentments, especially toward his mother. Something about being in a living body, though, released these chains, and he felt lighter and wished to move forward. But there was still one last chain he couldn't seem to shake. Nina could see it in those beautiful eyes—so close to being free, yet unable to make the final amend he so desperately needed.

He'd only spoken of Greta once, when they'd decided to take her room as their bedroom. *'If only I'd talked to her, said something, done something sooner, she might not be . . .'*

Remembering that moment, Nina eyed Colin as he spread out a broad quilt of yellow, navy, and gold octagons.

She kneeled with the picnic basket. "Holden, here, come help Momma."

"Help," the toddler echoed.

"He's getting so good at talking." Colin lay down on his side and nibbled on a sandwich. "This is good, hun."

"Thanks." She smiled, helping herself to her own sandwich. "Wow, this honey is good. It's not sweeter, exactly, but different from before." Holden opened his mouth, wide and expectant. Nina chuckled. "Okay, little bird, you can have some too."

They ate in the shade of the old trees. Nina cleaned up their food while Colin and Holden horsed around. Colin tickled Holden, the child's giggling like delightful chimes in the breeze. Nina sat back on her heels, taking a mental picture of a moment she wanted to remember for years to come.

A little while later, Holden played nearby with a ball. He'd toss and scamper over, running headfirst and looking like a funny little bird, then pick it up and throw it again. Nina and Colin lounged on the quilt. Together, they looked up at the sky.

Nina gestured to a cloud. "Tea cup?" she mused, resuming a game they'd often played the previous summer.

"Mmhmmm," he approved. Then Colin pointed at a particular fluffy cloud passing overhead. "Honeybee?"

She playfully jabbed him in the ribs. Colin propped up on one arm and leaned over to kiss her. Nina ran her hands through his golden hair. His lips were as soft and sweet as the first time they'd kissed. No, sweeter—sweeter, yes, she thought, because we belong to each other.

Colin pulled back and looked into her eyes. "Are you happy?"

Nina frowned. "Why ever would you think I was not?"

He waved a hand at himself, and the surrounding orchard. "I would understand if this were all too strange for you."

Her hand was still in his hair. She tugged him closer and kissed him fiercely. "I love you, Colin Richardson. We're a family."

Colin smiled in a way that warmed her to her toes. "Good." He stood, dug something out of his pocket, and got down on one knee. "I know you're considered legally married to this physical form, but

in spirit . . ." He blushed. "Nina, would you
marry me?"

Her eyes lit up. She squealed with excitement.
"Yes, yes, I will marry you!" Nina hurried to her feet
and threw her arms around his neck. They kissed
for a long time.

Colin broke away, laughing. He held up the ring
so she could see it. It was a gold ring in the shape of
honeycombs, each set with a diamond that winked
at Nina in the sparkling sunlight. "It belonged to my
grandmother," he said, slipping it on.

"It fits perfectly." She lifted it up, admiring it in
the light. Her elation deflated a bit. Nina bit her lip.

"What is it?" Colin asked.

Nina turned and stepped toward the ancestral
trees. "It's too quiet . . ." she said. Anxiousness became alarm, her joy becoming fear. "Where's
Holden?"

Deafening buzzing brought Nina and Colin to
their knees. They clamped their hands over their
ears. Nina was the first to regain her composure. She
yelled to Colin, but he shook his head, unable to
hear. Nina looked from him to the trees. She
sprinted into the heart of the four crones.

"Holden!" she shrieked at the top of her lungs.
Nina could barely hear herself over the oppressive
droning. "Holden!"

She whirled at the center of the trees, not far
from Greta's headstone. All at once, the life that
flowed through the orchard halted—the leaves hung
stiffly from the branches, the grasses no longer
swayed gently in the breeze, the air hung limply
against her skin. The buzzing roared and then—

—broke, receding, giving way to the natural
sounds of the orchard.

Her heart thumped in her chest as if a rabbit were stuck in her ribcage. What was this? This had happened before, last summer; it had been Colin. Was this John? Did he somehow figure out how to possess the bees when they took his essence from his body? Her mouth poised to cry out. Where was her son?

Grass crunched nearby. Colin burst through the underbrush and hugged her with a desperate tenseness that rivaled her own. "You haven't found him—"

Giggles.

Giggles issued from the shady depths of the eldest tree.

Colin released Nina, and she took a tentative step in that direction. The leaves parted like a curtain. The shadows stirred. Nina spotted silver and black streaks first. She stepped closer, taking a shuddering inhale. It couldn't be.

Greta emerged from the grove, stately as ever, cradling a happy Holden in her arms. She approached Nina and handed Holden to her.

Nina studied the red line of her lips, her aquiline nose, the slight disdain in her brow. "Is it really you?"

The old woman smiled and opened her arms. "Yes, child."

Nina rushed into her arms and hugged Greta. "I missed you so much," Nina whispered. Then she pulled back and wiped tears from her eyes. "How dare you do that for me!"

Greta *tsked* her. She pinched Holden's chubby cheeks. "There was no way I was going to let you leave this angel."

Nina embraced the old woman once more.

"Thank you. *Thank you.*" Pulling away, Nina made room for Colin to draw near.

His lips quivered. He fell to his knees before her and wrapped his arms around her waist. "Mother. I'm so sorry. Can you ever forgive me?"

Greta used two slender fingers to lift Colin's chin. She brushed his hair out of his eyes. Tears slid down his cheeks, and Greta brushed those away, too. "Forgive you, child? I'm your mother. There is nothing you could do that I wouldn't forgive. I'm just happy to see that you've found happiness."

Holden wiggled in Nina's arms. She let him down to run over to Colin, who picked him up. Nina joined them under the watchful protection of the four ancestral trees. The faithful sun warmed the land, the dark cloud hovering so long over Orchard Hill was no more.

THE END

Want to read more *Hopeful Horror* stories? Don't miss the chilling southern gothic tale *The Haunting of Willow Creek*!

FREE SHORT STORY
You can't escape its grasp...

Concerned about her moth-
er's unsettling phone calls,
Samantha returns home
from abroad to find the curtains drawn and the win-
dows nailed shut.

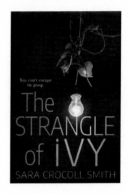

Is dementia causing her
mother's strange behavior
or something much more
sinister?

*Claustrophobic humid-
ity... creeping ivy... dark
secrets...*

Samantha's been the perfect daughter her entire
life. As she uncovers what lies at the heart of her
childhood home, she'll never be the same again.

**Visit SaraCrocollSmith.com/Ivy to get the free
short story "The Strangle of Ivy."**

LEAVE A REVIEW

Did you enjoy *The Haunting of Orchard Hill* and want more like it? Consider leaving a review!

Reviews greatly help other readers discover the book and let me as the author know you crave more hopeful horror stories. Even a sentence or two makes a huge difference.

Thank you so much, my spooky friend!

ON WRITING THE HAUNTING OF ORCHARD HILL

Part of me doubted whether this day would come—that I would hold in my hands a completed, published book that I'd written. For years, I drafted books and got so very close to the finish line before finding a reason to get swept up by something else, to not polish it and ship it out into the world.

When I got pregnant with my son, I was so excited. Yet in the back of my mind, I wondered about my dreams. If I couldn't make them work before, what made me think I could make them happen while caring for a baby?

Oh boy, I had *no earthly idea* the challenges that lay ahead. Shortly after returning to work and my son starting daycare, the pandemic began and I found myself back at home, juggling telework and full-time care of an infant. Luckily, I have the most amazing husband in the world and we somehow made it all work. But every waking minute consisted of working or being with my son.

I felt myself slipping away. Writing fiction is how I process the world around me, my emotions, my life. I, like most authors, can get quite cranky if I go too long without writing. I had to get creative.

During those early days with my son, I spent a lot of time on my feet, especially pushing him in a stroller. I may not have had uninterrupted swathes of time to type, but I could talk. I *could* dictate.

And so, I told my son a ghost story during the fall of 2020. You may not be surprised to discover that I was very much exploring what it means to be a mother as the novel is deeply interwoven with this theme. It captures a special essence of that first year with my son and I'm so thrilled to be able to share this story with you.

As an aside, however, this is a work of fiction. While it has imprints from me and my life, it is by no means autobiographical. For example, my husband is nothing like John. This book may be dedicated to my son, but every book I write will forever be dedicated to my husband. He pushes me to be even more of who I am and has not once questioned whether I could accomplish my dreams. I love you, babe.

To all my family and friends who've supported me throughout the years, thank you from the bottom of my heart. You have no idea what it means to me.

I loved writing this book and hope to write many more haunted tales. If you want to get notified of future books, make sure to sign up for my *Hopeful Horror* newsletter and get the free short story "The Strangle of Ivy" at SaraCrocollSmith.com/Ivy.

THE FASCINATING LORE OF HONEYBEES

When researching to write this book, I was amazed at the rich history and lore surrounding honeybees.

Honeybees are said to have a connection with the afterlife. In fact, "telling the bees" of a loved one's death may have origins as far back as Celtic mythology.

Many of the details regarding singing to the bees in this book are based in real folklore, including draping the hives in black and the dire consequences of not telling the bees of a death in the family.

If you want to learn more, these two articles are good places to start:

- JSTOR Daily "Telling the Bees"
- Wikipedia "Telling the Bees"

If you enjoyed this melding of nature and ghosts, you don't want to miss the free short story "The Strangle of Ivy" at **SaraCrocollSmith.com/Ivy.**

ABOUT THE AUTHOR

Sara Crocoll Smith is the author of the ghostly gothic horror series *Hopeful Horror*. She's also the award-winning editor of *Love Letters to Poe*, a haven to celebrate the works of Edgar Allan Poe.

For an exclusive morsel of gothic ghosts and daylight horror, visit SaraCrocollSmith.com/Ivy to get the free short story "The Strangle of Ivy."

ALSO BY SARA CROCOLL SMITH

The Haunting of Willow Creek: A Hopeful Horror Novel

Take from the Weeping Willow, and the Weeping Willow will take from you...

When Birdie arrives at Willow Creek Mansion for an artist's residency, she believes the grant could finally unlock her dream of a photography career. Yet she soon senses something sinister lurks on the southern grounds.

Fifty years ago, the contemptible benefactress disappeared, leaving behind her blood-stained will. The only instructions? Five artists of different disciplines must create works inspired by the eponymous willows of the area.

Is Birdie willing to pay the ultimate price for her passion?

Whispering willows... ghoulish paintings... slithering roots...

The foundation of Willow Creek is not at rest. As Birdie rushes to discover what's buried beneath, she'll be forced to trust what she cannot see and fight for more than her life.

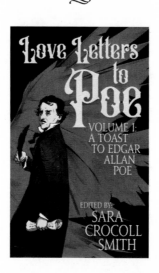

Love Letters to Poe, Volume I: A Toast to Edgar Allan Poe

An award-winning gothic anthology edited by Sara Crocoll Smith. Take a tour through Poe's Baltimore home, experience "The Tell-Tale Heart" through the old man's eyes, go corporate at Raven Corp., witness "The Fall of the House of Usher" from the perspective of a hidden Usher sibling, and much more.